Road To

Persepolis

Barbarian Tales

BOOK 4

www.BarbarianSpy.com

This book is copyright © Sabb 2010
First published by BarbarianSpy in 2010
Cover design by S Bush © 2010
Cover Photo © S Bush
Ebook ISBN 978-1-921879-07-4
Print ISBN 978-1-921879-08-1
All rights reserved.

Published by BarbarianSpy an imprint of Cyberworld Publishing
Jindalee St, Toronto, Australia.

Other books by BarbarianSpy

Not all books listed below may currently be in print release.

BOOKS BY DIRK HESSIAN

Blue and Gray
Colonel's Treasure
Beginning of Time
Prophecy of Noto
The King's Men
Labyrinth

BOOKS BY HABU

13 Ways for Halloween (Menage)
The Indian Prince
The Handyman
Grab Bag
Cairo Surrender
Fetish Galore!
Homeward Bound
Journey to Mirage
Choke Hold
Sporting Life

BOOKS BY SHABBU

Dirty Pool
Operation Black Jade
Yap, Yap
Cigars!
Angel in the Barn
Gayly Complicated
Despoiling David
The Tree of Idleness
Rough Road to Happiness
I Met a Man
The Interview
Rough Road to Happiness

BOOKS BY SABB

The Legend of Holleystone Grange
Surprise Encounters
She is He
Wrong Man
Loyal to his King
Barbarian Tales - Book One - Traveler's Tales
Barbarian Tales - Book Two - Journeys Begin
Barbarian Tales - Book Three - The Inheritance
Barbarian Tales - Book Four - Road to Persepolis

~

Road To

Persepolis

BARBARIAN TALES

Book 4

by Sabb

CONTENTS

Chapter One: Meeting the Merchant Vivana

As soon as I saw him I was distracted from the business I had been doing—discussing the final disposition of some valuable goods we carried—and that never happened. But with him it did. As soon as I saw him he took my breath away. All thoughts of anything else left my head.

He had approached my camel master, Malenos, and within minutes he was hired; before I even reached them, the barbarian was hired.

I trembled when the barbarian looked at me as I approached them, and I knew there would only be grief for me if I delayed the moment of truth. Yes, the great barbarian who had arrived out of nowhere had me burning with desire for him, a desire such as I had not felt for years. And if he was to travel with us, I knew he must satisfy it. Otherwise . . . he would have to go. "Send him to my tent," I said to Malenos as I passed them.

"Barbarian," I said, trembling and having trouble forming the words as he stood before me in my tent. "Welcome. Sit." I felt a bit more in control with him sitting down before me but had no idea what sort of man he was, or how to proceed, given he was fully armed.

And armed in every way. Armed with great beauty and size, with muscular strength, and a sword and bow that were not only of the finest workmanship but also meant for work.

"Greetings, Vivana of the Medes, I am Konan," he replied, leaving me quite confused, as he was obviously no illiterate savage from the wilds of the north, and the name Konan brought up in my mind thoughts of that legendary giant, famous among men.

"Greetings, Konan. I am not a young man anymore," I began, "but . . . there is a place for you in my bed . . . or I shall not need you and will pay you a portion and send you on your way." I had been blunt. We departed shortly, and I needed him gone or to know where his place was before we left.

The barbarian smiled at me. Not only did his golden hair hang in glossy waves to his ears, not only was his skin the color of honey, but also his smile was open and engaging, showing healthy white teeth and narrowing his eyes and making them glitter with interest. And he laughed, a low rolling sound that had my blood rush to my groin yet again, a thing I would have thought impossible, because my manhood already throbbed and ached at the very nearness of him. No man before him had ever had this effect on me.

"What you ask is possible, Vivana, but only if your bed is one worth lying in. And that I will only know by trying it first," he replied, looking at me with that open smile of his as he stood up, showing me his body in its full height, and took off his weapons and laid them aside.

"No, we leave shortly—within the hour," I stammered, but was unable to tear my eyes from him.

"I will know if I want to share your bed in far less time than that," he replied, looking down at me with a look of interest. "And if I don't want to, I will happily leave."

And with that, he untied his loincloth and let it fall. My mouth fell open at the last magnificent part of his form to be revealed to me and at the great size of the weapon that was growing between his thighs, matching in every way his muscular golden body.

He stepped over to me then and with his big, strong hands pushed me back on the rugs and cushions I had been seated upon and knelt above me. I found his mouth with mine, desperate for the taste of it as my hand reached for his manhood and grasped it, melting to its hugeness.

His kiss was sweet, yet overpowering. His tongue filled my mouth and possessed it as his hands ran beneath my robes and found my own throbbing manhood. He ran his long strong fingers along it gently, stroking it, discovering its veins and its root in my still-dark curls, and the end of it, and exploring in the small entry in its end, which one fingertip strove to enter. His strong fingers explored all of its length gently, yet firmly, sending me almost to the point of release, before those magic fingers moved to my sac and the two eggs it holds. He rolled them about and squeezed them lightly, tugged my sac gently, and rolled its contents yet again, before his fingers moved on, exploring the rest of my body. I knew he would find it firm and lean still. His other hand now lifted my head to him, and we could kiss endlessly as he knelt beside me.

Meanwhile, I had one arm about his neck, holding my mouth to his in that long kiss, while the other, trembling hand moved over his magnificent muscular body, first feeling the two muscular swells of his chest, each topped by hard excited nipples—that they should be excited as he kissed me, was yet another wild arousal. Then feeling the hardness of his ridged belly and the strength of his solid thighs, before returning to his manhood. Ah, its size, its hardness, its thickness. The strong, full, engorged veins writhing down it. I moaned, lost to him.

His fingers eventually found their way to my entrance, already quivering in anticipation of being invaded by the great club that throbbed between his thighs, encouraged by my stroking hand. He pushed my robes up, revealing my own stiff, throbbing lance, and I released the kiss to look down for a moment. Then I rested back on my elbows as he moved to kneel between my thighs and pulled me up and into his lap before he grasped my arms and raised me up till my chest was close to his, my belly feeling the hard heat of his manhood pressed to it, and then my own organ resting against his as I sat upon his great thighs. My mouth fell on his again as his fingers entered my well-used hole.

We had been stopped in the town for several days, and in that time I had tried the best men to be found there in the houses of pleasure, as well as those who came to find me hoping to gain some gold by showing their prowess. And I had thought a few of them were very fine indeed at taking command of me and using me well. But none came even close in size and commanding aspect to the great barbarian who now held me to him.

He chuckled a low rumble when he felt how loose I was, and I felt another finger, and then another enter me, to ensure I was fully stretched, while my hand trembled as it stroked his mighty sword, too big now for me to fully encircle with my fist.

He broke our kiss, and I looked down at where our bodies almost met between his thighs and mine. That great weapon of his was magnificent, thick, long, heavily veined, and slick, with precum beaded at the tiny entrance in its bulbous red head. I lifted my legs and wrapped them about his body, and raised my ass up, while looking down as he pushed off my stroking fist and placed my hand on my balls as he ran his fingertips up the sides of my throbbing manhood. I came, my seed spouting wildly up between our bodies to land on both of us, small drops falling on his chest and belly, and on mine, my body moving with the spasms of my spouting and my mouth making moaning cries.

Then he directed the head of that magnificent weapon of his to my asshole until I felt it rested there, my rim quivering at the pressure, eager, yet afraid still to take it in. Meanwhile he wiped my cream up off our bodies and removing the head of his phallus from my rim and, bringing it back into sight between us, he wiped my cream onto the head of his great throbbing club. Such a sight. One I will never fail to be overcome by the memory of.

Then that slick bulbous head was back at my rim, pushing harder at my entrance, and he pulled my hips to him, demanding access, as I found his mouth. For though I was well used, I wanted that kiss to stop the sound of my cries at the pain of his entry, for he truly was a giant.

Ah, and it was an entry such as I had never experienced before, and even my slack hole was tested before it fully opened to him and eagerly pulled him deep inside me. There was some pain indeed, but it was a moaning for the coming pleasure, pain. Then I felt the wonderful rubbing back and forth excitement, leading to returning hardness and finally to another spouting.

When I was ecstatically impaled on the full length and thickness of him, the barbarian lifted my hips and worked me up and down while I clung to his neck, gasping and moaning at the feeling of that huge weapon moving deep inside me, reaching my very core. For he touched places no man before or since has. And the power and depth of his taking made me weak.

My arms gave way, and he caught me as I fell back, and he lowered me to the floor, where I lay lost in his deep plowing as my hands roamed freely over my own body, rubbing nipples, stroking my manhood and belly, and looking up at that magnificent golden giant, watching his body rocked back and forth and his belly muscles creased and uncreased, as he pumped himself inside me.

At some point my camel master, Malenos, entered the tent, but I was only aware of his presence when he straddled my chest and presented his tool to my mouth. I sucked lazily on his familiar organ as the giant continued to plow my ass, but I pushed Malenos aside when I felt the barbarian was ready to come, so I could see his face. The barbarian lifted his hips, and me, off the ground and moved in and out of me in ever wilder twistings and turnings, finally jerking and stopping and throwing his head back and roaring like some magnificent animal celebrating his conquest over all. And as he roared, I felt his seed spouting deep inside of me. Then he held there looking down at me with satisfaction as I spouted again in turn, only a weak trickle but a spouting none the less.

When the barbarian finally pulled his weapon from my hole, there was a sucking sound, and his cum ran out and down my crease and thighs. I was lost to him, wanting nothing more than to be ridden again by him, and again and again. Malenos then moved in between my thighs and slid his own tool, wet from my sucking, into my gaping hole, while the barbarian moved to kneel above me and presented me with this great weapon to clean. I licked him lovingly, exploring his organ and taking in his juices greedily, while Malenos rode me furiously but briefly until his seed flowed to join the great barbarian's in my belly.

When Malenos pulled free, I looked up at the giant looming above me and murmured, "Will you come with us, barbarian?"

"Remember my name is Konan, Vivana, and yes, I'll gladly share your bed on the journey to the great city of the Medes, Ecbatana. But know that I am on the road to Persepolis."

"Konan. There is a legend," I murmured dreamily, "a legend of a giant . . . is that giant truly you?" I asked in wonder, for the stories were old.

"Perhaps," he replied, smiling at me. A smile that sent my blood rushing to my groin yet again. "Whatever the legend, know that I am named Konan and shall gladly journey with you, Vivana, to the capital Ecbatana."

I jealously kept Konan in my bed for the whole journey, something I had rarely done with any other man, for Malenos and several other of my men were well endowed and had great talent in pleasing me. They were jealous of the barbarian. But I did not care. None could compare to Konan, and I was greedy to have all of him before we reached our destination, and Konan worked himself in me alone. I know there was no other for him on that journey. But also he was not lazy and did the full work of a guard and camel loader also. Before we reached Ecbatana I begged him to stay with me, saying I would make him my heir. But he replied, "I thank you for the honor you do me, Vivana, for I know it is a great one. I am on a journey, though, and a merchant's caravan is no place for me for more than a brief time. I would have no heart for the life of a trader."

Then when we were but a day and a half from arriving in Ecbatana, we came upon two men I knew waiting beside the road beneath a group of trees beside a stream, where they knew I would stop the beasts for water.

"Greetings, Vivana," they hailed me when I rode up to them. "Come sit."

I had no choice but to join them. Konan came up shortly after to investigate, and I told him to join us, under the disapproving eyes of the two men.

"We are here on business, Vivana," one said. "Private business."

"No business of mine is private from Konan," I replied, wanting a reliable witness to whatever occurred, for I did not trust the two men.

"We have had no word from Felthe since the last moon, and you may not have heard that the body of the prince's catamite, Carpascus, was found at the bottom of a cliff, half eaten by animals."

"I had heard that," I replied, remembering the beautiful but foolish young man. "Both were young and foolish, and the concubine Felthe was arrogant and talked too much. What did you expect?"

"We expected them to arrive at Persepolis as they promised to."

"Their promises?" I laughed, "What good is the promise of an inexperienced child?"

"Neither was a child," they replied angrily, and it was not worth arguing with them. "You will have to go, now."

"Me?" I said in disbelief. "Why not you two? You are the ones who have not been able to manage a simple business like this. You are the ones who have boasted of what you are doing to half the world. If Felthe is also dead, it's as much your fault as her own."

"You vowed to fulfill a duty, Vivana," one said angrily. "If you do not, I will make sure you pay for your betrayal."

"Bah," I said, knowing the pair of them were fools and that I had been a bigger fool to ever get caught up with them. But that had not been my choice. No, it had been another's, one I owed a duty to out of respect for his father, and what his father had done for me when I was young.

"Enough," I said. "If I must, I will go to Persepolis myself, but the less you two know of my plans the better now," I said and angrily left them, with Konan walking behind me until we were out of earshot.

"I do not trust those two," I then said to him. "Old friendships and loyalties have got me into a difficult position, and now I may have to risk my life to get myself out of it, or more like throw my life away." With that, I mounted my horse again and went to check on the watering of the caravan's animals.

That night, though, as I lay spent in his arms, I told Konan some of what lay behind the visit of those two men. A small part of the history of the self-proclaimed prince of the Medes.

Several days later, at the end of that journey to the great Medean city of Ecbatana, Konan left me as he said he would. On the last day I lay with him and he plowed me deeply and endlessly. But still the time came when even he had spilled all his seed and he could not delay leaving me.

Then I gave it to him, my seal, the only gift of use to him, his share of gold for his work on the journey he had already had.

"When I was young and beautiful, I made friends with many of the great merchants of this world, meeting them along the roads and in the great cities as I did. And sharing many of their beds," I told him, remembering well how I had used my body to help me rise to my own high position in the world. "And if you show this seal to them, they will treat you well and trust you, Konan," I said to him. I then gave him the names of the greatest men I knew and had him memorize them. For there were many dangers along the road to the great city of Persepolis and beyond.

"I thank you, Vivana, and I know the value of your gift and am made humble by your love, and trust in me."

"No, it is I who am grateful," I said, with tears struggling to flow from my eyes.

"In return, I ask you that I may perform the duty the two men wished you to undertake by going to Persepolis."

"No, no. It is too dangerous," I said.

But he demanded I allow him to perform the dangerous duty I had been asked to perform. One I was known to have been asked to undertake and knew I was now being watched for. It was one I would not have passed to any other man but Konan to carry out on my behalf, and one I knew no one would suspect him of being sent to perform. One I would not have given to even him if he had not already been heading for Persepolis. So, I agreed to his demands.

After I had watched him walk off into the crowded streets of the market of Ecbatana, I knew it was time I went among my family, the many nephews and second cousins and even third cousins, and found a young man to make my heir. Malenos would be bitter, but I had always known he did not have the talent to take my place and would never make a good merchant.

He had been sulking and scowling for the whole journey when he found he was forbidden my bed. He had been a good camel master and a reliable if dull lover but perhaps it was now time he also left me. I doubted there would be room in my bed for him in the future either if I found a suitable heir.

Having made these decisions, I sat in my tent and drank a rich red wine from the south, until it sent me into a dreamless sleep. I had met a great barbarian named Konan, a man I could never forget, and who I had trusted above all others.

Chapter Two: The River Crossing

It was late afternoon and the ferry was tied up at the stone wharf on the other side of the river when I arrived at the crossing, and I could see the oarsmen sitting there, on the other side, eating their dinner. As I was in no particular hurry to get where I was going, I relaxed, easing my own hunger with some of the spicy grilled lamb rolled up in flatbread that was being sold by a vendor who had his cart set up at the top of the shallow ramp leading from the road to the wharf. Then I sat down on the edge of the wharf, and with my legs dangling above the water, I ate and studied the town on the other side as I waited for the ferry to return.

On the far bank of the river stood a sizeable town, with several stone wharfs and large warehouses. Boats moved up and down the river, and a dozen or so were tied up, loading and unloading. Large houses and buildings stretched for some distance along the river bank in both directions as well as into the distance away from the water in the direction of the road east. To the east lay the great Persian cities of Persepolis and Susa, and beyond them, lay Ur and Babylon, set on the banks of the mighty Euphrates River.

With me, on the other side of the river, were a growing number of people and pack animals, wanting to cross over to the town. Behind us was a collection of mud houses, built within a short distance from the wharf and strung along the riverbank. Other houses and shops straggled away from the riverbank, back along the road that led into the river crossing from the west. From the land of the Medes and beyond to the lands of the Great Mogul.

The lamb was delicious, and I returned to the cart for more after I had finished, taking my place behind a young, obviously well-off young man, with gold earrings and armbands and wearing a fine striped linen tunic. He was dark haired, as were all the local people, and well built with a handsome face, the sort of young man I would enjoy taking in some quiet area out of sight, and my desire was stirred at the sight of him. Yes, removing that striped robe and exploring his channel was a most appealing thought.

"And where are you headed?" the vendor asked him.

"To Persepolis, I have an uncle there who—"

"An eighth of a darius," the vendor said, interrupting him before he got into his story. He then cried "next," as soon as he had the young man's money.

"I follow the road to Persepolis also," I said in a friendly manner, as the young man moved aside.

He replied, "A great city." But he said it while avoiding looking at me.

It was a manner I found often now that I was moving into the West. The manner of men who saw a barbarian and avoided him. Men who thought themselves superior, because they believed they were more civilized than any barbarian, such as I, could be. And men who were afraid of me, because I was armed and obviously strong, and they were fearful of any armed stranger.

The young man moved gracefully off with his food, and I took his place and handed the vendor a small coin from the well-filled purse that was attached to the waistband of my loincloth and tucked in to rest beside my manhood. But at the same time I overheard the young man asking a group of other young men squatting nearby how long the ferry would be.

"When they have finished their dinner," was the loud reply.

"So we must wait here, when our business is on the other side and evening is approaching, so they may eat," he said, with a show of arrogant annoyance.

When I left the food cart I saw him still facing the group of three young men who had been waiting at the wharf since I arrived. All of them were as well dressed as the new arrival, but the three he was talking too also had oiled and braided hair, as well as the gold earrings in their ears and gold armbands. And I knew exactly what sort of men they were, and what they were looking for, and that they had now found it. The new arrival moved away from them briefly to stand at the edge of the wharf and look across the river longingly, and I returned to my place, sitting on the edge, with my feet hanging above the water, as I ate.

One of the young men joined the well-off young man. "I am Darius, named for the great Persian king, and we have been waiting for some time, friend. But the waiting is easier if we share some wine. So my friends and I welcome you to join us. We will happily share our wine with you, and perhaps a game of stones will make the waiting pass more quickly."

"Pardon my manners, Darius. I am Kasra, and thank you for your invitation," the new arrival said in the slow country way, obviously glad of the offer of company. And he rejoined the young men, and they passed a cup of wine to him to drink from.

From the background I was aware that the three men and Kasra kept passing the wine between them. And I knew he was being made to feel at home, so that soon they were all acting like old friends and laughing as the game of stones was amicably won and lost.

Then I forgot about them as the ferry left the far shore, and I stood up to get out of the way of the crowd that now pressed down to the end of the wharf in hopes of getting a good position and getting on board first. It was obvious that everyone waiting would not fit on the ferry for the first trip back.

I watched as the crowd jostled roughly, and when the ferry had run out its loading ramp, I saw the laden donkeys resisting their owners' attempts to get them to walk down the plank and onto the wharf, as passengers eager to get off struggled by them and those in a hurry to get on struggled and shoved their way past them also. I was amazed that they didn't all end up in the river, but only one man fell off the plank, to much laughter from the crowd and swearing from him.

Finally, the ferry had somehow emptied itself and filled itself up again and could hold no more passengers or cargo, and the steersman shouted to the crew, who pulled the ramp clear of the wharf, and the ferry moved off across the river.

As the crowd of offloaded passengers cleared, I noticed that the four young men had remained on the wharf, drinking and laughing and playing stones, and were waiting for the ferry to return, as I was. When it came back, it unloaded in a calm manner and everyone on the wharf went on board in a far more comfortable way than the earlier passengers had and we found places to sit and spread ourselves out for the short journey.

When we disembarked on the far side, the four young men went off together, laughing loudly and still passing the wine between them, and I saw that Kasra was looking unsteady on his feet. I got directions from one of the boatman and then turned my feet along the riverbank toward the largest of the stone warehouses.

* * * *

It was obvious as soon as Darius spotted him that he was a naïve and foolish country boy who had somehow come into wealth. Most likely an inheritance. And like all foolish country boys who got a few gold coins in their purse, he was heading for the great new city of Persepolis to make his fortune. Which meant lose it all. Every gold darius coin of it.

It amused Darius that his name was the same as that on our coins.

Well, we could find a much better use for this young man's funds than that. A much better use—for us.

He was easy meat, as we soon discovered. Not only naive, but obviously made more foolish by having been sheltered and educated by a religious and overprotective father. Ahh, a very nice prize we had found for ourselves. And very fine looking. Lean, and no taller than Perviz, who was the tallest of us, and with the fine muscle of an active, well-fed, and healthy young man. But so naïve. There was a magnificent giant of a barbarian waiting at the wharf also. He was so well made and handsome he might almost have been the legendary Konan himself. And it was obvious the barbarian was also interested in our new friend. But the young country youth was too foolish to see it, and to see what a useful protector such a man would be on any journey, but saw only a barbarian and his weapons. Ha.

His name, the young man said, was Kasra, from Gasterjaen, wherever that place was, and his father had served the goddess Bast. Foolish man. He'd served the great mother and been too much a mother to his son. But all to our advantage. Kasra was reluctant to drink much wine at first, or to play stones for a few straws, but Darius quickly got him loosened up and enough drink into him for the youth to forget how much he had drunk, and to drink from the wine cup whenever it was passed to him—which was every second sip.

"No. No, this ferry is too dangerous," we had all assured him when the ferry finally arrived from the town on the far shore. And seeing the pushing and shoving that went on as people got off and on it, Kasra quickly stopped objecting to waiting. And by then we had already convinced him to come with us and stay for the night at a friend's house, and join us on the journey to Persepolis in the morning. When the ferry returned for its second, far-less-crowded, trip and we had finally crossed the river, Kasra was walking unsteadily, swaying from side to side.

We hurried him through the town, showing him the wonders of its shops and empty market places only briefly—for it was late now. And we rushed him along the road leading out of the town so he spent none of the money we now knew he had in a purse hanging about his neck. Already we were on the road to Persepolis, we assured him, as we left the built-up part of the town behind and arrived at Xerxes's imposing house.

"Welcome," that black-hearted villain greeted us. "And who is your fine young friend?" he added, all lewd looks and running a hand over Kasra's ass as he guided him into the courtyard and on into the main hall.

"Our friend is Kasra," Darius replied, throwing an arm about Kasra's shoulders and pulling him from Xerxes. "And he is joining us here for the night. Tomorrow we all leave for Persepolis together."

"Ahh. A good idea, young Kasra. The roads are dangerous for a man not traveling in a strong group. And these young friends of mine are very wise about the ways of the road."

Xerxes may make use of us at times and be a thief and usurer, but he had never ruined our chances with any new target. Then he pulled Darius aside and demanded 20 percent of whatever Kasra had on him as well as the full cost of a night's lodging. Darius argued, but with no luck, as Xerxes knew there was no other house we could take Kasra to without bringing trouble down on our own heads. "And it's a busy night, and he is a fine looking young man, so how about I have the use of him for half the night, to cover his lodging here, rather than take it from his gold?"

"We get half the money you earn from him," Darius demanded angrily, knowing what Xerxes would charge for a man to enter the virgin ass of a good-looking youth like Kasra.

"A quarter, and I'll discuss it no more," Xerxes replied sharply, and we all knew that the haggling was over.

Kasra had heard nothing of the negotiations and seemed to accept that Xerxes was a friend, and we continued to fill him with wine and to play stones as Xerxes's servants laid out a meal for us, which we made sure Kasra didn't eat too much of. And he was too full of wine now to take much notice, as men began to arrive and select their rooms upstairs, before they came and inspected Kasra briefly, touching him to test the firmness of the virgin flesh beneath his striped robe.

When his head finally fell upon the table top, the three of us, Darius, Perviz, and I, stripped him of his fine earrings and bracelets, the striped linen robe, his sandals, his cape, and, of course, his purse. Darius and Xerxes counted his gold out between them, and we immediately took our shares from Darius, while a servant shook Kasra awake and helped him up the stairs.

"Us, too," Darius cried, looking up the stairs after the departing figures. "When he has well and truly lost his most valuable possession, we shall have a share of him too."

As Darius and Perviz ate and argued and laughed, celebrating our good fortune at the table in the hall, I climbed the staircase to watch what happened to Kasra, the good-looking young fool. He was washed down briefly with cold water, which seemed to waken him, and his face was slapped lightly by the servants till his eyes opened fully, giving him an appearance of alertness. Then he was taken to the first room. Kasra began to ask in a slurred unsteady voice where he was and why he wore only a short wrap about his hips, and, when they arrived at the first room and he spotted the big man who was sitting on the bed stroking his organ to hardness, he struggled and demanded to be released. But he had drunk so much that his struggles were uncoordinated.

"Where . . . who. . . why?" Kasra half shouted. But the big man grabbed him and slapped him hard and threw him upon the bed, and when Kasra tried to get up and leave, the man slapped him hard again.

Kasra fell back, holding his face, looking even more awake, but bleating words that were hard to understand. He flailed about as the big man turned him over and pulled his hips up roughly and fingered his virgin ass. I was sure it was virgin, and Kasra had hinted as much himself, though he was too embarrassed to admit it. The drunken young man cried out loudly as thick oiled fingers were forced into his tight channel and plunged in and out to the accompaniment of his cries and uselessly flailing limbs.

In short order it was the big man's good-sized organ that was presented to Kasra's hole and driven in. Kasra let everyone know that this was thicker than anything that had ever been up there before, and the big man planted a hand over his mouth to quiet him, which only made the youth struggle more, much to the enjoyment of his attacker, I was sure.

The pounding Kasra got was not very long, and then the man was jerking as he spouted his seed deep inside the young man's belly. After that he collapsed over Kasra's back and a hand grasped the young organ and grunted because it was still soft. Annoyed, the big man called out and a servant came to remove Kasra. I had my own rod in my hand, I admit, stroking it at the sight of Kara being taken so roughly, and then seeing his young ass dripping the big man's seed.

I followed the servant and a weakly struggling, but too drunk to get away, Kasra to where he was sponged over with cold water again. Now he was sufficiently alert that he was complaining loudly and struggling with the servants holding him, and they quickly hurried him to the next room. Here two men waited. Kasra was fighting the servants more seriously now, and I wondered if he perhaps had overcome the wine, as some men can, and knew what was happening and would remember in the morning. But considering how much wine he had drunk, and his inexperience, I doubted it. It would certainly be bad for us all if he did.

I stayed just outside the door to the room and stood off to one side, peering in. This time there were two men, the first man being old and wiry, but obviously very rich, as he had a young, naked god in the room with him. A dark-haired, pale-skinned young man with braided hair and gold jewelry all about him, who obviously spent time carrying weights to build up his body and who had a great, fully engorged and erect phallus that would have looked good on a horse and made my mouth gape. I stroked myself more furiously and came from just looking at him and wondering what that great piece of his would feel like working inside me.

"He is drunk," the young god said with annoyance, shaking Kasra, who had suddenly gone quiet and seemed to be on the point of passing out.

"Ah, he's . . . he's just tired, the excitement," the servants stammered.

At the scent of trouble, Xerxes magically appeared from wherever he had been lurking. "Ah, but he has been building up the courage to be taken roughly and for the first time. He is bound to be dizzy from thinking of it."

"His breath smells of wine," the young god added, having sniffed Kasra's mouth. "And a short time ago we heard loud cries, as of a young man being taken roughly."

I could see Xerxes getting annoyed.

"Wine! But don't we all drink it, even me? A good dinner, wine . . . the simple pleasure of life. A way to build up our courage."

"Well, I am not happy, Xerxes," the old man said loudly. "You are getting too bold. Thinking you can get payment for the use of a drunk, however virginal he may or may not be."

The older man sat there relaxed, but looking coldly at Xerxes, who suddenly bowed his head and wrung his hands. This was most unexpected. Xerxes was a wily villain who bowed to no man and even had influence in the governor's house.

"My noble master, this is a most desirable young man, as you can see, and a virgin, I swear."

The young god was though at that moment running his hand up between a now-quiet and slightly swaying Kasra's ass cheeks, and after quickly fingering his hole, withdrew his fingers and sniffed and licked them. "I think his virginity is already gone, unless he spouts his seed from his ass," he said, smiling evilly at Xerxes.

Xerxes waved his arms and cried in horror, "No. No. I don't believe it! What has happened? I said he was to come to you first, my lord. I swear to you."

Kasra was standing still now, but he seemed to be leaning slightly against the young god, who now had a hand wrapped about the late virgin's manhood and was fisting it to see if it would rise for him.

Meanwhile, Xerxes was being berated by the older man, "But someone else paid you more than I offered, Xerxes. Didn't he? Who?" he demanded.

"No one! No one, master. I swear, if he did not come straight to you, it was a mistake, and I shall beat everyone responsible."

I felt the young god's eyes on me and glanced his way, seeing that, in spite of the wine, Kasra had grown respectably under the young god's stroking hand and also seemed to be leaning in closer to him, till suddenly their mouths met. I felt someone else's eyes on me and turned back just as Xerxes pounced on me and dragged me into the room.

"Here . . . here is another fine young man," Xerxes cried, as if he had found the perfect solution to the difficulty he was in. "You may have both for as long as you wish, master." My mouth gaped, and I tried to protest, but seeing the frightened look on Xerxes's face, I just stood there, stunned. I would be a fool to offend any man Xerxes was afraid of. "Yours, both of them, at no charge," he said, smiling broadly, and left the room, closing and bolting the door on the outside.

I was trapped. Young Kasra seemed to be making happy little mumblings and was now playing a hand over the young god's chest. And I was not entirely surprised, as I had had an idea that might be where our young virgin's interest lay. And I would have been purring myself if the young god had been handling me.

"Here," the old man ordered.

"But . . ." I started to protest—stopped by the look in his eyes. He looked angry. So I did as he asked before he might get any angrier with me. "You don't know who I am, do you?" he said with a laugh. "I am the king's messenger. And you are needed here," he added, holding up the half-hard organ that had been resting between his legs up to now. "Let me feel those young lips."

The king's messenger! A man who was to be treated as the king himself, and who could order any fate to befall any man who interfered with his duties. No wonder Xerxes was afraid of him. I hurried to kneel obediently between his spread thighs, and lifting his organ to my mouth, I sucked it in and did the best job I could of making love to it. Working it up to full hardness. And I must have done adequately, because soon his hands were buried in my braids and pulling my head back and forth as he moaned. I could hear other moans too, and the bed shook as something heavy landed on it.

"He is not virgin, and he is drunk, but he is young and good looking and eager," the young god was saying, and I could just see his mouth meet that of the old man whose organ I was sucking on. They kissed passionately for a long time, and the old man's grip on my hair tightened as he jerked me back and forth more furiously.

But a hand suddenly landed on my head and pushed me off. "No. No. Not so soon, Thuxra," the young god demanded.

"Ah," the old man sighed, still panting.

I saw his hand move to the young god and run over him as the young man kissed him yet again. "Watch," the young one whispered as the kiss ended, and I saw Kasra now gazing dazedly, as if hardly aware of what was happening to him, as the god lifted his legs up and exposed Kasra's tight hole to us.

What followed had me stroking myself so that I was hard and throbbing. The young god sucked a finger and then ran it around that tight rim, making Kasra part his thighs and move his hips to increase the pressure. And I was sure Kasra was dazed, because he was reacting instinctively but fast discovering things he liked. Then the young god's long tongue was lapping at that puckered rim, wetting the entrance down and loosening it, making it quiver noticeably under his attentions, at which the old man poked a finger into Kasra's channel. The young one sank in another finger beside his master's, as they kissed again, and they worked their fingers in Kasra's passage as the kiss went on. When they broke the kiss, the old man pulled me up. "You're the thinnest," he said, "and this one may no longer be a virgin, but he is very tight, so you will go first and open him."

I was indeed the one with the thinnest organ of us three, if not the shortest of us, and I moved between the two of them and up to Kasra's ass and entered him. Kasra made some whimpering sounds and moved his arms about, grabbing the sheets on the bed—but as I breached his first resistance, he arched and moaned in wanting, and I moved into him as slowly as I could. And as I entered him, I felt hands part my own cheeks and an oiled hand stroke over my hole and fingers enter me, making me shudder, for I had turned my head, and my mouth was taken by the young god's. Ahhh.

I held still as he moved that great manhood of his to my entrance and pressed it in. I gasped and cried out as I was impaled by it, spreading my legs and leaning over Kasra to ease the young god's entry till my mouth met Kasra's and I began a deep probing kiss he lazily joined with me in, to cover the initial pain of having that huge organ move deeper into me. When the young god began to stroke in and out of me, I felt overcome and moved my hips in wild desire. I was totally stuffed and taken, wonderfully taken. And I came deep inside Kasra, as the young god continued to stroke inside me slow and shallow.

Then my invader pulled me back and sat me in his lap, still impaled on him and being lifted up and down on that immense organ of his, while the old man, Thuxra, took my place before Kasra and drove his own tool in. My seed leaked from the hole he entered and I moaned and moved helplessly up and down as I watched Kasra arch again and throw a leg wide behind the back of the young god on whose lap I rose and fell. Thuxra worked the young man hard. He then withdrew, still not having come.

I was lifted off, suddenly empty, and the young god moved into the place Thuxra had just vacated before Kasra as I was again pushed down to suck on Thuxra's erect organ.

The young god's entry to Kasra's hole was not as easy as ours had been, and the old man took hold of one of Kasra's legs and ordered me to take the other, pressing them wide. Having felt that great pole enter me, I sensed that Kasra didn't try to stop the young god from proceeding. In fact, his cries were more of desire than fear.

When the young god had pumped him hard and filled Kasra's channel with his seed, the old man pulled his lover to him. And I again fucked Kasra, as Thuxra fucked his lover. The old man came at last, his jerks obvious and vocal, and afterward the two of them fell together on the bed and pushed Kasra off it, onto the floor.

Falling to the floor didn't seem to affect Kasra; he simply lay there looking dazed. The thud brought Xerxes rushing in, though, and seeing the two men cupped together and kissing languidly in afterglow, he grabbed hold of Kasra and me and dragged us from the room and closed the door.

"You will take this . . . this . . ." Xerxes sputtered, kicking the prostrate Kasra in the ribs, "away from here now and leave him dead and well hidden, as far from here as you can," Xerxes hissed at me as I recovered my robe and put it on.

I woke my companions and tried to explain Xerxes's demands to them, but they were still full of the glow of a successful day and mellow from each other's explorations and were not paying full attention, until Xerxes himself grabbed them by the hair and dragged them from his house to the gate where Kasra lay.

We left Xerxes's house with Kasra tied over the back of a donkey, because he had now definitely passed out from too much wine and his exertions. And in the faint light before dawn, we hurried off along the road to Persepolis. When Darius was tired of the slowness of our progress because of the load the donkey carried, he dumped the young man in a deep, water-filled ditch.

"He may drown there, but I'll not deliberately murder for Xerxes," he said. "We will be long gone before he is found—and if he lives, well, a penniless beggar in a ditch will find no one to listen to his wild story or help him."

Chapter Three: An Overnight Stop

"I have the seal of the trader Vivana and seek your master, the great merchant Utana," I said to the supervisor.

In my travels about the world, I had long ago learned the value of having friends among the merchants and traders and was fortunate to be a friend of one of the most highly regarded of them, Vivana of the Medes. And I used his friendship wisely on my journey to Persepolis.

When I had entered the warehouse, he had been there, by the door, a small, wiry man wearing a blue robe showing he was a supervisor, though his skin was as dark as wood and wrinkled from the sun, as if he was a laborer. And it was him I now addressed. The supervisor looked me up and down and, without saying anything, hurried off, out of the entrance and back onto the roadway that ran along the riverbank. I followed him into the next, much smaller building, where he entered a side room and whispered to another man and left.

"Come with me," this new man, a scribe, said, and I followed him up an earthen staircase and onto the flat, low walled roof of the building. An awning was strung up over part of it, and beneath it another scribe sat on a low stool before a small table marking a clay tablet with a stylus. A wizened old man in a red robe stood at the edge of the roof, looking down at the river and the wharves. My guide whispered to the man standing and watching the river, who was obviously Utana, and then hurried away.

"The ten-oared boat returns from the north with timber," Utana said, "Bardiya's boat. If he has any long cedar tree trunks suitable for columns, we will buy them from him. They are needed for the governor's new house." At these words, the scribe wrote upon the clay tablet before him.

Then the merchant turned to me. "Your business, barbarian."

"I am Konan. And I carry the seal of the trader Vivana of the Medes. I journey to Persepolis, and he recommends me to you. I will take work as a guard, if the work suits me," I told him.

Utana considered me for a moment, "Show me the Mede's seal," he demanded politely, his sharp eyes never leaving me as I fished the small cloth-wrapped piece of clay out of the leather purse attached to my loincloth. What I held out to him was Vivana's seal, the small piece of clay he had pressed his ring into and given me so that I would be trusted by Utana and any other merchants and traders I met on my journey west. The other seal he had given me was separate.

Utana, the Persian, took the seal from me and inspected it in the sunlight, then handed it back. "It is Vivana's impression," he said with more respect. "He is a man I trust, barbarian. And I have heard the name, Konan, spoken before. So I will tell you that a caravan left my warehouse this morning, at first light, and that the next to leave will depart in four days' time. If you will wait, they will be glad of a guard such as you and pay you well."

"And the one that left this morning?" I asked.

"If you are in a hurry to reach Persepolis, you can catch up with them easily, as they have camels and are slow moving. But they had as many guards as they needed. I have no doubt, though, that they will feed you if you travel with them, as a guard such as you is always useful. But I doubt they will pay you wages."

I considered the choices. "I will go after the departed caravan in the morning," I replied, "as I would rather continue my journey than wait here."

Utana considered me for a moment. "I value Vivana's friendship, barbarian, so I shall give you my seal as he has. And you may sleep in the warehouse tonight, if you choose. See Jamshid, the supervisor you have already met, to arrange it." Then he took off the ring he wore, bearing his own seal, and handed it to the scribe, who laid a small piece of damp clay upon the table he worked at and pressed the ring into it, creating for me another guarantee of welcome. "If you show this at the house of Artostes tomorrow night, they will give you a bed indoors, and you will catch up with the caravan early the next day."

"I thank you, Utana, and know that Vivana will be glad of the honor you have shown me," I said politely.

"Go in peace, Konan," Utana answered and returned to his study of the river.

If it had not been early evening already, I would have left the town immediately, for I was keen to be on my way. But I had walked for many days, and a comfortable night's sleep under a roof was welcome. And Kasra, the wealthy young man at the wharf, had reminded me it was time for other pleasures also.

I returned to the warehouse, and, showing the supervisor, Jamshid, Utana's, seal, I advised him I would be spending the night there. But he looked as if he still had no liking for me.

"There is a guard here at night," he said curtly, but then smiled. "I will let him know you will be returning and that you may sleep here, friend," he added, now quite cheerful, as he showed me a rough mattress of straw laid out in a small side room.

"I have your master's seal," I reminded him, when I saw the rough accommodation he offered me. "I will have the visiting merchant's room as mine, Jamshid, not the laborer's. Show it to me."

Jamshid scowled at me and, muttering, led me to a staircase and up through the upper level of the warehouse and then up more stairs and onto the low-walled roof. Up there were three good-sized airy rooms with a covered shade in front of them, and inside the rooms were large, clean beds made up on wooden frames.

"I shall take this one," I said, choosing the best-appointed room. "And bring me water to bathe in," I added.

"Certainly . . . master," the old man replied sarcastically, and scowling angrily, he left me.

I removed my weapons and my blanket, unrolling it and placing my oil pot by the bed, and lay down for a brief rest, finding the bed most comfortable. And I decided to rest there a while before going out in search of an evening's pleasure.

I awoke in darkness to find both my arms above my head and feeling something snaking about my left wrist. My left arm not having been tied off properly yet, I heaved myself up and pulled my arms down so hard I heard the timber of the bed frame crack. And my right arm suddenly came free.

I swung my arms about then, aiming to hit whoever had been trying to bind me to the bed, and felt a jarring impact as if I had hit a solid wall. Then strong arms grabbed me, and I kicked back, hearing a grunt. I spun about and rammed my shoulder into the black, moving shape before me, but thick arms grabbed me again, pulling me in close. I was crushed to a hard, sweating body. A hard rod hitting my belly. I swung my arms again, and the timber I had broken from the bed head, which was still attached to my wrist, hit something solid. This time whatever I had hit let out a loud grunt and fell against the bed and to the floor. I jumped back and looked where the body should be and could see only a dark, moving shadow. I kicked it, and it was hard. And I heard a groan.

But then I saw them. Two white eyes, seeming to roll about, against the darkness of the dark shadow. For a moment I wondered fearfully if I was in the presence of some demon of the underworld. In my childhood my father had warned me of spirits that came in the night to take you away to join the ancestors. And my first fear was that such a demon had come for me. And I swore it would have to defeat me if it wished to drag me from this world into the next.

However, I quickly realized that a demon should not be lying there groaning and that its smell was a man smell, and that what I had felt on my belly was a man's organ.

"Are you a man?" I cried, kicking the shape again. "Speak. Or I shall kill you now."

"Stop, stop, barbarian," it howled. "Do not kill me," it wailed fearfully. "I am Doma, guard of this warehouse."

"You attack me, Doma. While I am a guest of your master, sleeping in your master's house, you attack me," I replied angrily, undoing and finding the lengths of cord he had been trying to tie me with, and finding Doma's arms in the darkness, I roughly tied them together.

"It was a mistake," Doma whined, as he struggled to move. "I thought you were an intruder."

"No," I hissed, "You wished me harm, Doma."

I was now searching for a light, still not able to see this man who had tried to bind me. Still seeing only a dark shadow.

"No, no. A mistake. A mistake. I thought you were an intruder," he cried out loudly.

"Yet you knew I was a barbarian, Doma."

"I . . . I . . . call all intruders barbarians," he stammered.

Finally I found the oil lamp and lit it. Now I could see. But what I saw amazed me. Doma was naked on the floor, and he was still black. A man as dark as night. A massive man, his body muscular, with heavy shoulders tapering to a small waist and hips, and massive thighs. And between those thighs lay an engorged weapon bigger than any I had yet seen on any man but myself.

"What sort of man are you?" I gasped in wonder. "Are you from the land far to the south? From the dark land?"

"I am Doma of the Nubians," he replied, still lying on the floor and holding his head, which had a small trickle of blood on it. "And I meant you no harm."

"You come naked into my room with your manhood erect and throbbing, Doma. And you try to tie me to my bed. Ha. There is no doubt what you intended, Doma."

"Jamshid, Jamshid," Doma cried loudly, "He said I could have you. He wanted to watch me take you."

If I had been angry before, I was now beyond anger, and I grasped Doma by a leg and an arm and lifted him and threw him across my bed.

"And where is Jamshid now? You have called him here, and he thinks he can watch. But Doma, it is you he will watch being taken now," I growled.

"No. No," Doma was crying, but I took up some bedding and stuffed it into his mouth and, tying his legs together in spite of his struggles, rolled him over on his belly. The great mounds of his ass quivered and glowed in the light of the oil lamp. My own manhood was growing at the very sight of him. And I reached my hands to stroke myself as I admired the black body of the Nubian giant before me.

But then Jamshid was coming through the door, and I moved quickly to capture him.

"No," he screamed as I took him by the throat.

"So, you wished to see me taken by this black giant?" I growled at him.

"No. No," Jamshid cried as he struggled and shook with fear. "I . . . I heard noises. I came to see what was happening. The Nubian is a liar."

"If you want to live, you will obey me," I whispered in Jamshid's ear, as Doma made strangled sounds and struggled against his bonds.

"Yes, yes. I will obey," Jamshid said, nodding his head furiously. "Anything, anything."

As he was nodding, I reached for the second leather cord that had bound my blanket and lashed his writs together.

"No. No, not me. No," he howled, and I tore off his robe and stuffed it in his mouth.

Then I dragged him to the bed and tied him to the frame. He was a thin man, but the organ hanging half engorged between his legs was surprisingly long, if thin. And pulling the rag from his mouth, I pushed his head down to my filling weapon and ordered, "Suck." And with my hand at his neck, he did. His tongue and lips performed a wonderful dance and quickly brought me to throbbing hardness. And while Jamshid worked, I admired Doma's body and his ass. Two massive mounds of hard muscle that glowed and rippled in the light of the oil lamp.

Doma had turned his head, and wide eyed, watched Jamshid at work on me. And his eyes slitted, and he was moving his hips slightly before I finally pushed the warehouse supervisor off me and I removed the bedding from Doma's mouth.

"So tell me, Jamshid, why did you and Doma attack me? Did Utana order you to? If you tell me I may treat you gently."

"No, no, it was not Utana," he cried in distress. "It was a mistake," he moaned.

Then I joined Doma on the bed and his eyes opened wider, and he tossed his body about and struggled. But that did nothing but leave him breathless.

"Please, no," he cried his eyes fixed on my engorged weapon. "Know that no man has taken me since I reached this land." And as my hand moved between his cheeks and I pressed a finger to his rim, its tightness and firmness told me he was at last telling me the truth.

Jamshid knelt wide-eyed now, looking at Doma and me, and I could see his own excitement growing.

"Tell me then. Why? And what did you want to steal from me? Was it your master's seal? Or was it Vivana's seal?"

"Nooo," Doma wailed in fear, as Jamshid hurriedly said, "I only came because I heard a noise. I know nothing."

I doubted Doma would talk with Jamshid there, so I got off the bed and took up Jamshid's robe and tore a strip off it and bound it over the supervisor's eyes. Then keeping his hands tied together I released him from the bed and dragged him up, out of the room and onto the open roof.

"Tell me why you attacked me, or I shall throw you off this roof, Jamshid. And if I do, I doubt you will be able to tell anything to anyone ever again. And then without you to silence him I will discover all from Doma."

"No, I cannot," he wailed.

I pushed him against the low wall about the roof. "Feel the wall against your thighs, Jamshid." He writhed and struggled and begged me not to push him over.

"Tell me," I demanded as I pushed him forward so his chest hung over the wall then pulled him back, teasing him.

"Who?" I hissed in his ear.

"A merchant's man. He came past three days ago and said to search all who came this way and who know Vivana. To search them for a seal and to destroy it. There is a reward of 100 Darius for the pieces of the broken seal. That is all I know. I swear. We meant you no harm. We were going to tie you up and search you and then leave you. We meant you no harm. In the morning thieves would be blamed, and you would not know who we were. That is all. I swear."

"And whose man was it who came?"

"I cannot say, I cannot," Jamshid whispered in obvious fear.

"Was it Gaubaruva's man?"

Jamshid went rigid then. "No, no. I don't know. I don't know," he cried, but I knew he lied.

I did not believe he and Doma had meant me no harm, but the rest I did believe. I dragged him back into the room where Doma lay tied on the bed, his eyes big and fearful.

"Now I know all, Doma," I said as I tied a protesting Jamshid to the bed frame again.

"So you will let me go," he said hopefully, relief flooding his face.

I jumped up on the bed above Doma and roughly lifted his hips high, so he was on his knees. He struggled to widen his thighs, but I set a leg each side of his, pressing his legs together between my thighs, to the sound of his moans of, "No, no. I cannot . . . I cannot."

"I had intended to go out and gain myself some pleasure tonight as I have spent many days on the road, and desirable bedding companions have not always been at hand in the night. But I see before me now, Doma, the man I most want to take my pleasure with this night, and another who will enjoy watching. You have saved me the trouble of leaving this comfortable room."

"No, no. I cannot." Doma moaned,

But I knew he could. And would. And a pale Jamshid looked on with slitted eyes, not seeming too displeased with the sight before him.

I applied oil to my hard, throbbing manhood and parted Doma's firm, round cheeks and ran a finger into his channel. He moaned. I added another finger, and he resisted me. But I ignored him and forced it in. He whimpered at my invasion of his body. But my other hand had reached beneath him to feel the weight of his massive balls, and I felt his own organ growing hard beneath him.

I entered Doma then, while he cried out. He was tight, and made tighter by my thighs holding him close. Jamshid's mouth was gaping at the sight before him, and his own tool grew and stiffened making him whimper.

Doma's canal was as tight and muscular as the rest of him, and I took some time to work in fully, while he grunted and moaned. When I began to pull back, I felt him squeezing me tight. So I plunged roughly in, to the hilt, and he howled. When I withdrew again, his canal quivered on me, and I moved back in less roughly and repeated the motion of in and out, in and out, in short strokes, until I felt his channel open to me. Then I was stroking in long slides, in and out, almost completely out, and then in again. He had a fine ass.

And he was soon helplessly muttering strange words and moving his hips with mine. I continued my plowing for some time until he came, his canal caressing me as his seed spouted onto the bed beneath him. Then I drove deep and released my own seed fully inside him, throwing my head back and roaring as I came. When I withdrew, my juice dribbled from his gaping pink asshole. And I heard Jamshid moaning and turned to see him spouting his own seed in big gobs up his chest.

Soon after, I untied Jamshid and ordered him to stroke himself to hardness again. Then I had him mount Doma and enter him, his thin manhood sliding effortlessly into that now well-stretched hole. And as he began to work inside Doma's channel, I got up behind him.

"No, no," he cried in fear, as I pressed my hand between his thin cheeks and two fingers up into his passage.

Finding his spot, I rubbed my fingers over it, and he, was saying "no, no," but was also moaning and continuing his pumping of Doma's ass.

Doma was now joining the rhythm, and when I had entered Jamshid's ass canal, which was looser than Doma's, both men were lost in the joining.

Later I moved Jamshid off Doma and took my place again inside the Nubian giant.

By now Doma was begging, "Suck me, suck me," and I released his wrists, and he reared up and threw his arms back around me and we kissed. Then he turned over and Jamshid immediately dove on his black friend's enormous tool and began sucking it noisily.

I ran my hands over Doma's magnificent body and toyed with his nipples and stroked his belly and then cupped and gently squeezed his balls and he came, his great body jerking several times as he filled Jamshid's throat with his cream.

I worked Doma's willing ass from every direction then, and Jamshid sucked any weapon that was free, and I had no need to leave that room to enjoy a night of pleasure.

I awoke at dawn, with my manhood still buried in the great Nubian's ass, and after working my reengorged organ in the sleeping Doma and filling him with my cream one last time, I withdrew and left them there. The great Nubian guard, Doma, his hole gaping and leaking my cream, and the supervisor, Jamshid, both on my bed, pressed skin to skin and still asleep.

Outside the streets of the town were becoming busy as I walked back along the riverside until I reached the road to Persepolis. I joined it where it began at the stone wharf where the ferry was tied up, and followed it toward the west.

When I had left the houses of the town two, or three, miles behind, I came upon two farmers staring down at something in a deep ditch beside the road. I stopped by them and saw what had stopped them, a naked, dirty man lurching up and then falling back as he tried to get himself out of the ditch. All the time groaning and wailing.

"I think he may be mad," one of the farmers said.

I doubted it and straddling the narrow ditch I leant in and pulled the man up by his hair.

"No. Not mad. Drunk," I said.

The well-off young man from the wharf was now naked, dirty, poor, and very drunk. He vomited as I held him up and then tried to speak to the farmers peering down at him and to shake me off.

"I am from Gaster . . . Gasterjaen. Everyone . . . everyone there knows me. I have . . . have an uncle in Persepolis."

"I think that I will leave him here," I said, dropping him back into the ditch and returning to the road.

"No, no," he cried, struggling to get up and out onto the road. "I must . . ." He turned and was sick again and swayed. "I must . . . my friends. I must find my friends." He looked at the farmers for help, but they were laughing and hurrying off.

Finally, he looked at me.

"I need. . . to get . . . out of here. Help me out," he said to me as if I were a servant.

I looked at him.

He reeled, then steadied himself, and after a short while said "Please . . . help me out of here . . . barbarian."

"My name is Konan."

He struggled yet again to get out of the deep ditch but fell back again. "Konan," he finally stammered holding out his hand to me. "Pl . . . please help me out of here."

I grasped his hand and pulled him out onto the road, and he collapsed there. I looked down at him for a moment, and then I continued my journey and left him lying there.

Soon after I heard noises behind me and turned to see him staggering wildly about the road as he tried running to catch me.

"Don't, don't leave me," he stammered when he caught up. "I . . . I . . . have noth . . . nothing." His lips quivered and tears started to run down his face. "I woke up and they were gone. And everything, everything of mine was gone. I . . . I think they took it. You have seen them. The three of them. Come back with me. I need to go back and find them. My . . . my gold, my . . ."

I shook my head. "You will never find them, Kasra, and if you do, they will have some story of thieves, or of you leaving them and going off alone, that makes them innocent. And I am on my way to Persepolis."

Chapter Four: Kasra's Awakening

I remember very little after getting off the ferry with my three new friends. We had been drinking wine and playing stones on the wharf on the other side of the river while we waited for the ferrymen to finish their dinner and return. On their first crossing of the river, the ferry was badly overloaded, and the crowd was rough and rude, and we had waited for them to come back again.

Darius, who had originally invited me to join them, and his friends, Ashkan and Parviz, were all well dressed, with brightly colored robes, gold jewelry, and fashionably oiled and braided hair. I envied them their hair. Mine was growing now, but while my father lived, it had always been kept short like a country boy's. My father had been a strict man. At the wharf, the three of them had seemed very agreeable company, and we were all heading for Persepolis.

Once the ferry arrived in the town on the other side of the river . . . well, I remember very little. I do remember them telling me they had a friend whose house they stayed at. A friend who had food and a bed for them all, for a small fee. I knew no one in the town, so it seemed like a generous offer by them to let me join them there, and when we arrived, I seem to remember the house looked large and prosperous.

But I soon had the idea it might be an inn or business of some sort, as men were coming and going from the upper floor, and some came and asked me my name. But I remember little. Just bits. And even now I do not remember anything between when I was sitting at a table in that house with my new friends, drinking wine, playing stones and winning, and when I awoke the next day.

I shudder still at that awakening. Ah. But for me that morning was the beginning of my awakening in many ways. So, though I shudder, I am also glad that I woke up as I did, if that makes sense to anyone but me. But my first awareness of that new day—what a horrible feeling it was.

I awoke because something was digging painfully into my side, and the pain got so unbearable it dragged me from my stupor. But as soon as I moved, my head seemed to fall off my body and spin about. Oh. And waking I felt more pain. Very oddly there was great pain in my ass, and pain in my legs and my arms, as well as sharp things digging in to a hundred places on my body. And there was a cold wetness numbing one side of me also. I tried lifting my head and opening my eyes, but the light was blindingly bright, and my head felt as if it rolled off again. And the indignity of it. For as I moved, my belly rose up in me, and its contents came out of me. I felt like dying.

I wailed loudly, hoping someone would come and wake me from this bad fever dream I was in. For at first that is what I thought it was. But no one came, and the dream didn't end. I was soon aware enough to discover that I was naked and dirty and that the cold wetness I felt was water lying in the bottom of the deep ditch I was lying in.

I think I howled even more loudly then.

For some time I cried for help and wailed at my misfortune to have been somehow set upon and left there, and I vaguely even worried about my three friends' fates. Yes, I was that foolish. Occasionally, heads peered at me over the edge of the ditch, and I cried out to them, but they all quickly disappeared. I struggled to get out of the ditch also, but the sides were steep and muddy, and I was hardly able to stand up and too unsteady and sick to manage it. And at times I lay there sobbing. For I also knew that all my goods and gold were gone. The gold I had carried on me that my father had spent his life accumulating—gone in a night. And I wailed and railed against the gods. But I also begged the goddess Bast to rescue me.

Then, as the sun rose higher, I saw a great blond head peer down at me. A barbarian's head. I cried out in fear that to add to my troubles I was to be killed, or worse, by a barbarian. I fell down yet again as I was struggling to escape up the other side of the ditch, and he straddled the ditch and pulled me up by the hair, as the faces of two other men appeared again.

"Help me, help me. I from Gaster . . . Gasterjaen. Everyone . . . everyone there knows me. I have . . . have an uncle in Persepolis," I shouted up to them, hoping they would save me as I struggled to escape the barbarian's grip. But then my stomach heaved again, and I threw up a thin trickle of bile and they disappeared. I tried to pull free of the barbarian and could not help looking at him and realized I recognized the man holding me up. He had also been at the ferry wharf the evening before.

"I think that I will leave him here," he then said, letting go of my hair and dropping me back into the water.

"No, no," I cried, struggling to get up and out onto the road. "I must . . ." I turned and was sick again and swayed. "I must . . . my friends. I must find my friends," I rambled as I looked up at the other men who were back again, only to see them look at me as if I was a madman and then turn and hurry off.

Finally, I looked at the barbarian. After all I was still alive and he was the only one there.

"I need . . . to get . . . out of here. Help me out," I said, hating to have to speak to him.

But he just looked down at me as I looked up at him.

I steadied myself, "Please . . . help me out of here . . . barbarian."

"My name is Konan," he replied.

I struggled to get out of the deep ditch and fell back again, hating to have to ask a barbarian for anything, but it was useless I had no choice. "Konan," I finally stammered. "Please help me out of here."

He knelt down and reached his hand to me and I grasped it, and in a moment I was out, on the road. I collapsed there and tried to gather my wits. When I looked up, it was to see Konan walking away from me. And I ran after him. Well, I staggered.

"Don't, don't leave me," I stammered when I caught up, gasping for breath. "I . . . I . . . have noth . . . nothing."

I tried to still my quivering lips and stop the tears that ran down my face, but could not. "I woke up and they were gone. And everything, everything of mine was gone. I . . . I don't know where . . . my friends, they will know . . ." but it was dawning on me that perhaps they already knew exactly what had happened to me. "Perhaps . . . perhaps . . . you have seen them. The three of them. Come back with me. I need to go back and find them. My. . . my gold, my . . ."

Konan shook his head. "You will never find them, Kasra, and if you do, they will have some story of thieves, or of you foolishly leaving them and going off alone, that makes them innocent. And I am on my way to Persepolis."

I was shocked he knew my name.

"How . . . how do you know my name?"

"I was there when you met your friends at the wharf," he replied, turning and heading away from me again.

I lurched after him, covering my nakedness, nothing in my mind now but getting to Persepolis and my uncle's house. I knew no one else, except those back in my village, and that was farther away, and I had promised myself never to return there.

I almost lost sight of Konan several times and my feet were badly scratched and bruised and I was nearly exhausted when I found him at midday resting under a tree, eating.

I collapsed on the ground by the road and watched him. There had been others on the road, but no one had wanted to listen to me when I tried to ask their help, though some had grabbed at my manhood and made immoral suggestions, until a man had handed me a rag, which I had gratefully wrapped about myself to cover my manhood. "My uncle will reward you, Konan, if I arrive safely in Persepolis . . . I know it, for he is a wealthy man."

He looked at me. "You are a fine-looking young man, and if you please me, you may accompany me," he replied.

"I will try hard to please you," I told him, suddenly overcome by relief.

"So, come here and please me, Kasra," he replied.

I looked at him in confusion, "What do you wish done?" I asked, not thinking of anything I could do for him just then as he looked quite comfortable and was eating well.

After a minute he laughed and, getting up, handed me a strip of dried meat and walked off. I attacked the meat, my belly aching for food, and hurried after him.

He did not slow down for me, but I was able to keep up better as my head cleared and my body recovered from whatever had poisoned it earlier. Then, when we came to a wide stream, Konan stopped and walked a short way up from the ford to a deeper pool and said, "Now we bathe," stripping off his loincloth and wading out into the water. I hurriedly removed the rag I wore and carried it into the water with me, meaning to clean that too, and scrubbed it hard before I scrubbed myself with it, pleased to rid myself of the filth that covered me still.

It was a while before I looked at Konan. But when I saw him, my heart almost stopped. He stood thigh deep in the clear pool, and water ran down him as he reached his hands up and back to wring the water from his golden hair, his body stretched out and glowing in the sunlight. He was magnificently formed. Ah. He might have been some god as he stood there for that moment.

And I wondered how I had not seen before how handsome he was. Suddenly, I felt myself redden and turned away and scrubbed myself harder to cover my embarrassment. My manhood had begun filling at the sight of him, as it did at times at the sight of men, though I tried hard to stop it. For my father had warned me sternly against such things.

Shortly after, I could not stop myself glancing over my shoulder at him, though. And Konan was running his hands up and over his belly and down into his bush to slide along his manhood, which was standing hard and erect, and . . . I quickly looked away. He had been looking at me and seemed to be smiling but with slitted eyes. But in spite of my efforts, I could not stop my own sword from stiffening, painfully in need of release. I ached to stroke myself but could not while he was there. I hurried to wring out the rag and leave the water. But before I could step onto the bank, I felt a hand wrap about my belly and stop me. I quivered at the touch and almost fell down. And then the other hand, Konan's big, strong hand, moved down to my throbbing, aching organ and wrapped about it, easily covering it entirely, even the tip of it.

I whimpered and collapsed back against his firm body. But I moaned, "No, no . . ." as he began to move his hand up and down my length. Behind me, I felt the hardness of his own great sword pressing against my lower back, moving up and down also, and in no more than two strokes of that great hand on me, I had spouted my seed into his fist and up my belly twice. As I recovered, I tried to pull away from him, but that hand, almost covering my belly, held me there as his other hand moved behind me and between my cheeks.

I had heard of what unnatural things men did with other men. My father had told me they were evil, so I had stayed away from those who might do such things. Now I shivered at what the great barbarian might do to me, as a finger pressed at my entrance, and "Ouch," I grunted as it entered me. "Oh," I added involuntarily, for I was for some reason very tender and sore there.

"Your friends have stolen your virginity as well as your gold, my young friend," Konan said and laughed a low, rumbling laugh that vibrated through my whole body, making me quiver.

I was horrified by what he'd said. "No. No, they would not do such a thing. No man would. I remember nothing, I . . ." But I knew that my ass had been sore all day and realized there had been more than exhaustion making me stagger.

Konan withdrew his hand and released me, and I scurried up the bank and wrapped the now-cleaner rag about me. I could not look at Konan. I was totally confused and mortified.

Soon I was hurrying along behind him again though, as he strode down the road.

Later in the day, when we arrived at a small town, Konan asked for the whereabouts of the house of Arestos. Finding it, he showed the wary man at the gate what he said was a merchant's seal. And once the man guarding the gate saw it, he was all eagerness to please Konan and hurried him in to Arestos.

"You and your servant shall sleep in one of the bedrooms I keep for visiting merchants," Arestos said, giving me an appraising look.

"The stables," I muttered, frightened of what sharing a room with Konan might mean. "I am quite happy to sleep in the . . ."

Konan turned to me. "You agreed to please me," he said. And indeed I had, though I now had some idea that pleasing him might involve far more than I had ever imagined when I gave that promise.

But before I had to worry about anything else, we were well fed, and all other thoughts fled my mind. It seemed to my simple country-boy experience that a royal banquet was before us, and we were joined by Arestos and another visiting merchant as we ate. I was ready to eat a whole beast alone, I was so hungry, but my stomach was still delicate, and I was quickly full and falling asleep at the table.

I was sent up to our room, escorted there by a young serving woman, who kept giving me sidelong glances and whispered, "You are so lucky. And if he tires of you, tell him to ask for Amira," as she left me. I blushed at what she seemed to suggest, then I looked at the large well-made bed and was so tired I removed the rag I wore and fell across it, instantly asleep.

I remember nothing more till I woke to find the great barbarian lifting me like a baby from the bed and laying me gently on a mat on the floor. I was still only half awake but quivered with anticipation and fear at what he was about to do to me. But he did nothing. A few minutes later I heard another man enter the room and then the sound of a man's body hitting the bed. I turned my head and saw the other merchant who was staying there kissing Konan and pulling him down to him, and the barbarian climbed up and pinned the man beneath him as his mouth held his eager lips. My own manhood stiffened at the sight, and I could not stop myself stroking it as I watched Konan roughly part the man's legs and finger his ass, as he had mine in the stream. But now he added more fingers as the man arched and twisted and grasped the bed frame.

And when Konan was ready, he drove that huge organ he possessed into the man's asshole. The man cried out and, grasping his legs, pulled them back and wide before Konan leaned in, and they kissed again, to the sounds of their bodies meeting and the bed groaning and banging with each deep thrust Konan made.

I stroked myself and came before either of them did. Then I stroked myself again and watched Konan move the man about and onto his chest and lift his hips as he worked his great weapon even deeper in him. And I came again as the man cried out and fountained over the bed beneath him. Then I fell asleep.

Konan woke me, and I looked up bleary eyed as his hand squeezed my shoulder. I sat up, finding a folded robe of good material and a pair of almost-new sandals beside me. Then saw that he had sat down on the edge of the bed with his legs spread.

I barely glanced at my new clothes, my eyes were pulled instead to his huge phallus rising up his belly, emerging from his golden bush, with his big balls hanging beneath it, between his thighs. He was stroking that great club with delicate fingers as he looked at me, and he said, "You can go with a robe and sandals, and a full belly, or . . . ," and he signaled me to go to him. I got up, my eyes fixed on that great weapon of his with a burning desire to touch it. And with my heart pounding and my breathing ragged, I shuffled over until he gripped my arm and pulled me between his thighs.

My own manhood was growing and stiffening even as I moved to him, and his other hand now stroked me and cupped my balls till my organ was also hard and standing erect. Then he pushed me back a step and dipped his head down so his lips encased the head of my cock, sucking briefly, before moving down my shaft until his mouth briefly enveloped my manhood. I moaned and clasped his hair in amazement. The feeling of that warm embrace, ah. Then his lips were gone, and he pulled me in close again, his mouth finding mine and pushing my lips apart and his tongue entering me. I let him. I admit, I welcomed him. And as my hands ran over his magnificent muscular body, I understood that whatever my father had warned me against was what I most wanted.

I felt him possess my mouth, and then I felt him plant a finger between my ass cheeks and slide it to my hole. I quivered as he pressed the tip of it into me and hesitantly moved my arms about him. Then he moved me away again and reached for the small oil pot by the bed and, pouring oil into his palm, dipped his fingers in it. Then he pulled me in, and our hard organs met, my smaller one sitting next to his much larger one. And I felt the hot hardness of it, as it was resting against my belly, beside my own. I reached for his manhood, my hand barely covering half of it, and he kissed me again, this time long and demandingly as I ran my hand all over his massive club.

Then Konan turned me about and had me bend over, facing away from him while resting my elbows on his knees as he parted my ass cheeks and worked the oil into my channel with his fingers. They were so thick that as the first one snaked deep inside me and moved about, I felt filled just by that. It was an amazing feeling as that finger found the magic spot inside me that made me moan when he rubbed it. But then another finger joined it. I felt pain at first as he entered and stretched my channel. Once he had worked the two fingers deep inside me, I arched back and moved my ass about, eager for them to stroke every inner part of me, and moaned loudly.

Sometimes I could feel the head of Konan's erect organ brush my ass, and I shivered in anticipation of that great rod working its way inside me as it had been worked into the merchant the previous night. Now he pulled me up and moved me so I lay back on the bed, my eyes overcome by the sight of him between my thighs as he pushed my left leg up to my chest and knelt before me. Soon three fingers were inside, stretching me painfully. The pain lessened when he stroked my belly and cupped my balls and squeezed them gently. Then my ass was empty.

"Don't stop," I begged, "Don't . . ."

I heard a deep laugh rumble in his chest as he took the oil pot again, but this time he pulled me up and filled my palm with the oil and then drew my hand to his great maleness. His throbbing, thickly veined manhood rising up from his golden curls, and his big full balls. I shivered in understanding and wrapped my hand about him and stroked the oil all over that throbbing pole, which was soon to be digging deep inside me. Awakening me.

I wanted to take him all. To be totally stuffed, as even his fingers hadn't been able to make me feel. I knew that was what I wanted as he pushed my legs back and apart and moved in closer between my thighs. And stuffed I was to be. Gloriously stuffed. Crying out as he invaded me, before he clamped his mouth over mine and roughly took possession of it again.

He stopped once he had got past my first tight resistance, and I painfully, yet slowly, accepted him, and he was able to move deeper. And then I felt a feeling such as I had never felt before and my moans were no longer just of pain and I threw my arms about him and pulled him tight to me wanting him deeper, wanting him to posses my body completely.

And amazingly he did. But it was a slow progress, and I came twice before he had his bush pressed to my ass, and I held him there, my arms embracing him tight as I gasped at the feeling of that huge weapon filling me. And then he plowed me, at first gently, and hardly withdrawing, but then in long deep slides until he threw his head back and roared. And as he roared, I cried out, because I felt his seed exploding deep inside me. And my awakening to my manhood was complete, as my own organ erupted yet again.

Chapter Five: Meeting an Old Companion

My caravan was large, fifty camels loaded with crates and sacks, containing fine fabrics, spices and herbs, oils, ceramics, and cord. Ten donkeys were pulling the carts loaded with our own supplies and iron tools for trade, and there were two small horses for me to ride. Thirty men traveled with me—camel drivers, carters, and strong men who also carried arms, whose work was to load and unload the camels each day, to frighten off timid bandits, and to fight off serious ones. And my old cook, Hooman.

The rear guard, Dashan, brought the two men up to me where I rode at the head of the caravan. We had been on the road for only three days, and there was almost a moon to go before we would be within sight of the gates of Persepolis. This was the new capital of Persia, where the great king, Darius, was building a magnificent new city full of temples and palaces, a suitable center for the great Persian empire he now ruled. And a merchant knows well that where there is a great king building a new city, there is always plenty of money to be made by a trader bringing expensive fabrics and fine baubles for the palace hangers on and their wives, as well as tools for the craftsmen. And Persepolis might be a great city for kings and princes, but it had no great bazaar and was many miles from any other city with one.

The two men made an odd, yet appealing pair. One was a magnificently built, tall, and muscular blond barbarian, who stood proudly before me, while the other was a dark young man of great beauty, who stood shyly just behind him. "They wish to speak to you, master," the rear guard, Dashan, said eyeing the two men warily but respectfully. "The barbarian says he has the seal of Utana, who he also says sent him after you."

"Greetings, Melioc," I heard a voice saying, and I realized it was the barbarian who spoke.

"Greetings, stranger," I replied courteously, surprised that he spoke so well and addressed me as an equal by my name. The few barbarians one saw about who were dressed in loincloths were generally recently come down from the hills and rough, small men, most suffering from a shortage of good food and with no education. But this one was obviously an exception in every way. "Show me the seal," I demanded, wanting to know if it was true he had it. Few men had ever been given Utana's guarantee of trust, and this barbarian did not look like one who would be.

"Here." He unwrapped a cloth parcel he held and handed one of the two small clay objects it contained to me. "I come with the seal of Utana, but we are not strangers, Melioc," he continued, as I inspected the small piece of clay. "For we have met on the road before and traveled together. But I was young then, and not the man I am now, as it was not long after I had left my village."

He paused as if I must remember him, but I didn't. I had made many journeys and many men had traveled with me—some for a day, some for a lifetime. I merely examined the seal in my hand and wondered what the other piece of clay he had was. For what I held certainly was Utana's seal, which few men had ever been given, and I handed it back to him. "I'm sorry, I do not remember you. Did you work for me once? I am sure I would remember if you had, for you are a giant. What work do you and your companion have experience in?"

"I am called Konan, Melioc, and I have been a caravan guard before," he said, then indicated the young man behind him. "This man, Kasra, has no experience, but he travels with me."

I looked at the barbarian with new eyes, for like all well-traveled men, I had heard of the legend of Konan. "I have all the guards I need, Konan, but as Utana recommends you, you and your friend are welcome to travel with us and shall be fed, if you agree to help when needed."

"So be it," said the barbarian. I signaled to Dashan to return to his work, and my caravan continued on its way, the barbarian and his friend walking beside me.

"Perhaps it will help you to remember me, Melioc, if I tell you that you gave me good advice on our first journey together. Advice that I failed to take. I was young and my first destination when I left home was to be the sea, but after a few days on the road, I met you, and you offered me the protection of your caravan for my journey, as you too were headed for the sea, to the city of Tyrins."

I looked at the barbarian, and my mind recalled several young barbarians I had taken a fancy to at one time or another on a journey to Tyrins and the sea, but they did not connect in any way with this golden giant. The barbarian youths had been of average height and lean, though one who had died had been very alluring and precocious. But this man before me was a massive man, full of confidence and maturity. "Ha," I laughed. "I would certainly remember if I had ever met a barbarian as massive as you before."

"Ah," he said smiling, "But I was not as I am now, Melioc. We came to a pass between two mountains. There was the white of snow high up on the mountaintops, and I asked you what the white was. You told me it was solid water and—"

"You? You were the one who asked why the gods would make water solid?" I was shocked. "That barbarian was a wild precocious one, a young, slight man. His name . . .

his name, his name . . . yes, it was Konan, yes. I remember him. He went up the mountain, and I never saw him again. But . . . but, he was nothing like you. I remember that. I asked after him on the following trip, and the local people said that the old men on the mountain had died and that two young giants had left there with their dogs. Some thought they were the old men magically returned to their youth."

"Cedric and I were the young men who left there with the great dogs, Lycos and Anubis," the barbarian said. "And you have a good memory, Melioc, to remember the young man I was before I went up that mountain and came into the care of those old men, in that ancient temple. I am Konan, and I thank you for my life and greet you."

I looked at him, still confused, because it was not possible to imagine that young, lean Konan becoming this magnificent giant. But there had been stories about the magic of the old men in the temple. "And where did I meet you?" I asked him, wanting to be sure.

"Where?" He shrugged. "On the road. I caught you up and asked if the road led to the sea, and you could not understand me until I spoke slowly."

I had been studying his face for some sign and then remembered how his hair had been blond and had hung about his face, framing its youthful beauty. And as I looked, I could see that frame of golden hair about this man's face still—and the beauty of his face. A different beauty, though, not a fine, lean, youthful one, but a strong, muscular, manly one. "Yes," I said finally. "Yes, you are the same Konan. Ha, and I have heard tales of a great barbarian called Konan, who . . ." and I laughed, for I had often wondered if the stories of the great barbarian Konan were real or imagined, never dreaming that I had once perhaps had that same Konan, a lean and beautiful youth, lying in my camp for several nights and driving me wild with unsatisfied desire.

"Well met, Konan," I said at last, and, sliding from my horse, I embraced him. "Well met indeed. It had deeply distressed me to think you had died on that mountain. We saw the storm coming and had to shelter from it, seeing it sweep over the mountain you had climbed, hiding it in a dark mass of cloud. But tell me how you have grown to be such a giant of a man?"

And as we traveled, Konan told me of how he had come upon the temple high up on the mountain as he was near death, and of its inhabitants, and how he had been healed by them, and how the healing soup had made him grow strong and tall.

And I saw there was some deep sorrow there too, though, because he talked little of the others in that place. This time there was no wild desire in me to have him, but I could not help but look often at the young man who accompanied him. He was indeed beautiful, young and lean and with an open and innocent air about him.

That night, when the camp was set up, the two of them joined me in my tent for the evening meal. They knelt, and plates of meat and vegetables were spread on the carpets that covered the dirt beneath the tent.

Kasra seemed unsure how to eat the food we had, and I rolled some lamb in a leaf and, moving closer to him, I tentatively held the parcel to his lips. I could not help myself, even though Konan, his master, and I was certain, lover, was there. When he had eaten it I sat back, feeling I had gone too far, my cock having grown hard at the very feel of the young man's breath on my skin as his full, luscious lips took the food from my fingers.

"I take Kasra to his uncle in Persepolis. He is young and honest, but too innocent to make his own way in the world yet," Konan said then, looking at me as if warning me off. "That is all I know of him, Melioc. But while he serves me, I shall guard his safety on the road and deliver him to his uncle."

I felt foolish, knowing I desired no more than to have the young man in my bed because he aroused me, in spite of him and his master being my guests. "Your worldliness surprises me, Konan. So tell me, where have your travels taken you since last we met?"

"Far to the east, Melioc, as far as the prison of the Great Mogul."

I gaped at him. "You have traveled that far? What great wonders have you seen? Ahhh, to have the time to trade so far and bring back the fine artifacts I have seen that come from there."

"Wonders? Few. The mogul's army is strong, and his palaces are large and luxurious, but men are men, and powerful men are often dangerous to be about," the barbarian replied. And I could only wonder at the simple but polite manners and understanding of the world he had gained since we first met.

But my eyes returned often to Kasra as he ate in silence, seeing the young man gazing often at Konan as if fascinated by him, like some puppy. At the end of the meal, I gave them each a woolen robe to wrap about themselves at night. "The journey will take us to places that are cool at night. These will warm you," I said, passing them each a robe, my hands brushing Kasra's skin as I did so and that touch sending a fire through me.

They ate with me each night and then left my tent to sleep with the other men, about the fire, beside the camels, or among the crates and bundles of my merchandise. I should next have seen then in the morning as they helped to load the boxes and sacks upon the camels. But instead, when the fires were doused, signaling the men that it was time to sleep, I silently crept from my tent and found the place where Konan and Kasra slept. And each night I crouched in the shadows and fisted my hard throbbing organ to release, as I watched the great barbarian take his beautiful lover Kasra.

Kasra served the barbarian with his body in every way he could. With his mouth, his tongue, his lips, his hands, and by giving Konan's great weapon entry to his sweet hole. From my hiding place, I saw immediately that all the stories of the barbarian's great size were true and wondered in amazement at Kasra taking that thick, long organ. But take it he did, gladly and often.

As soon as they were alone, they kissed deeply, hands sliding all over each other, each teasing the other's chest, rolling nipples and sliding over asses—Konan's fingers teasing at Kasra's chest and with his cock and balls before Kasra knelt and took Konan's great, hard manhood in his hands and guided its head to his lips, playing them over it before opening wide and sucking the first few inches of it in and working it in and out. Then Konan would turn him and push him down onto his knees and tongue his entrance, then oil his fingers and finger Kasra's wetted entrance briefly with one, two, and, finally, three fingers, as the youth moaned and moved his hips in harmony. Then I could see the oil glisten and drip from the young man's hole and run down his inner thigh, and know the barbarian was about to plunge his huge club inside that very hole.

Or Konan might have Kasra stand before him, as the barbarian knelt down, taking the young man's balls and upstanding manhood gently into his mouth, as he reached a hand between Kasra's parted thighs and his thick, long fingers searched between his cheeks and disappeared into his ass, finger fucking him as he sucked. Kasra moaning and writhing, his knees going weak so that it seemed it was only Konan's fingers buried in his passage, and his other hand palming his chest, a small nipple caught between two big fingers, that held him upright. Then Konan knelt and Kasra was lowered onto Konan's huge organ as the giant guided its bulbous head to that tight, but well-oiled hole. The young man's legs widening impossibly as Konan's mouth took his— their kiss stopping Kasra's cries as his body shuddered and descended slowly on that huge pole, their kiss breaking only when the young man's ass was buried in Konan's lap.

I could tell when Kasra was totally stuffed, and then he'd be lowered back so his shoulders lay on the spread robe, and he looked up at his master. And only then would Konan begin to move his hips, drawing his manhood out of that sweet channel, then pushing it back in, while Kasra writhed and arched his back and his hands toyed with his own nipples and slid to his hard throbbing manhood as Konan cupped his balls and played with them.

Kasra moaned and writhed as he lay back, but his moans were of pleasure more than pain when Konan entered him and plowed him. And Konan would rotate his hips and drive hard before throwing his head back and roaring as he came deep inside the young man's belly.

Then one night, as I crept nearer, I heard sobbing and almost stumbled over Kasra sitting behind two large sacks.

"What is wrong?" I was shocked to find him there, and deeply worried.

"No . . . no, I can't."

"Come, tell me," I urged him, and not seeing Konan about my hand moved to his shoulder.

"Konan, he . . . he is with two other men. I must no longer satisfy him," he sobbed. "Tonight he has not taken me, but he has gone to two other men."

I was surprised by Kasra's distress and deeply moved by it. Konan was right, he was too innocent to make his way alone in the world. And at that moment, I wanted to take him in my arms and kiss his slender body from head to foot, my tool engorging at the thought of his naked body beneath me. I shivered at his nearness and could not stop myself. "Shush, shush, it's all right," I murmured as I bent my head and placed my lips on his in a kiss. At first he accepted my kiss, but then he shook me off.

"No. No. I am with Konan," he cried and scurried away.

I was left there, aching for release and almost overcome with desire. I couldn't help myself—I hurried after him. No matter if I told myself I dared not try to take what was Konan's. Or knew that if I wanted Kasra, I would have to take Konan's place as his guardian and lover.

For me, a free man, it was unthinkable. If I loved—it was easily and with no bonds. I was not a man wanting to protect and be faithful to any man. But Kasra had me under a spell, and I could not stop myself. I found him further along the line of crates and sacks, his knees pulled up to his chin, still sobbing.

"Shh, shh," I whispered, sitting next to him and wrapping my arms about him and rocking his slender body against my chest. "Shhh, a man has needs," I said, having no idea what to say. "And Konan is a man with legendary needs. No one man can satisfy him."

I moved a hand to Kasra's lap and stroked him. I pulled him closer to me and whispered sweet words in his ear. I told him how beautiful and desirable he was, and how any man would want him. And as his tears stopped, I found his mouth with mine again and kissed it.

Ahh, the sweet taste of him. And I felt his organ growing, hardening under my stroking hand, as mine throbbed and ached for release. Our kiss grew deeper as my tongue entered his mouth, and I shuddered as I pulled his hand to my weapon, which he only had to stroke hesitantly for me to spill my seed. Then my hand encircled his growing organ and began to bring him to a softly moaning release, but he didn't spill his seed for me.

There were noises, and the sound of Konan calling, "Kasra," softly, and Kasra pulled away from me. Forgetting me in an instant, the name "Konan" on his lips as he ran toward his master.

I was left there, abandoned, and torn between lust and respect for Konan's legend and Utana's seal. There was half a moon still before we reached Persepolis and I had no idea what the power of my desire for Kasra would do to me in that time.

Chapter Six: Kasra Finds His Voice

Kasra was lying there beneath me after I took him, and I knew that the time I had spent away earlier that night, with two of the camel drivers, had distressed him. And in the afterglow of our fucking, he gazed up at me and mumbled, "Melioc, he . . . found me. While you were . . . gone. And he . . . he—"

"What, Kasra? Did Melioc take you as I do?"

"No, no," he hurried to assure me. "No . . . but he touched me, and I . . . I touched him. Can you forgive me?" he asked, looking distressed.

"There is nothing to forgive," I replied, but I also felt it was time young Kasra spoke of his pleasures. That he admitted to his desires in words, as well as with his body. For not being able to talk of his pleasure in lying with me was to deny a part of it still.

"Come Kasra, tell me what Melioc did."

"He . . . he . . . he, kissed me."

"Ah, is that all?" I said with a chuckle, being sure there was more.

"No, no. Not all. He touched me too."

"He touched what, Kasra? Your lips?" I said, kissing him and then placing my hand on his engorging young organ.

"Not my lips, well, yes, my lips, but . . . me, that . . ."

"All the things we do have names, Kasra, so tell me what I now hold in my hand."

"My, my . . ." he stammered bashfully, "My organ."

"Do you mean your cock?"

"Yes, yes."

"Say it for me. Say what Melioc did."

"My cock. Melioc touched my cock."

"Ahh, like this?" I said, stroking my hand over the full length of him.

"Oh. Oh no, not so well as that. Ahhh . . ."

"And what did you do?"

"Me? Well, he took my hand and made me touch him."

I laughed softly. "So tell me exactly what he did, and I will do it. Then you may tell me what you want me to do, and I will do it. I want to hear you speak of it, Kasra. I like to hear the words of our joining. To listen to a man describe what we do and ask for what he wants."

"Melioc took my hand to his manhood," he said, wrapping his hand about my engorging organ, "and I stroked it," he said, stroking me. "He is not so big as you are, and he quickly spilled his seed."

"Shall I spill my seed quickly?" I asked him.

"No, no," he replied, pulling his hand away.

"Then I will not," I said, pulling his hand gently back to my now well-engorged weapon. "And then what did he do to you?"

"He stroked my cock as he kissed me, but I did not . . . spout my seed."

"Ah, why not?"

He hesitated. "Because I heard you call me."

I bent to kiss him, the sweet young man.

"Now tell me what Melioc might have done next, if you had not heard me call you, or what you would have me do to you now."

"Now I am hard and eager for you to move your hand to my ass, and . . . and . . ." he laughed in embarrassment. "And you move a finger to my entrance and . . . yes, ahhhhh, you push it inside me."

"Inside where?" I asked, teasing him by moving my finger about as if searching for somewhere to lodge it.

"Into my hole," he said and guided my finger to his entrance. "Yes, in, then deeper."

I nudged him. "Deeper into my channel," he added.

My finger entered him and stopped. And after a moment he looked confused.

"You are not moving it, why?"

"Because you have not told me to," I replied, holding my finger steady just inside his asshole.

"Move your finger about, as you usually do, so it rubs that special spot inside me," he said in a rush, as if the muscles of his tongue had finally been freed. "Yes, like that," he moaned as I rubbed the pad over his hidden gland.

"More fingers, another," he moaned. "And you. Fill me," he paused, "plunge your sword into me. Hard and fast," he demanded.

"Are you sure?" I asked him, sure it would be painful for him, though I had already plowed him well and he was oiled and opened in there.

"Yes. Yes," he said as he lifted his legs, running them up my body, and I leaned over and kissed him on the mouth. Meanwhile, I guided my cock to his hole and plunged it in. My kiss stifled his scream, but his legs spread wide and wrapped about my hips, and he pulled his ass hard up against me also. We held there, me buried to the hilt inside him as I broke the kiss and he lay there panting and trembling.

Slowly he relaxed, and when he had finally adjusted to me, he whispered. "Long and deep."

"What is it you want, Kasra?" I asked him.

"Move in and out of me long and deep and hard," he ordered me in a dreamy voice.

I laughed. "Kasra, tell me in the words I want to hear."

"Move your great throbbing cock in and out of my asshole in long deep strokes, right in and almost out, then plunge in again."

"That is called fucking, Kasra, or plowing."

"Konan, fuck me, plow me, long and deep. Fuck me. Fuck me," he chanted rhythmically.

And I did. When I had spouted my seed deep inside his channel, he stopped me, pulling out with his thighs about my hips, and asked, "Was it better with the other men?"

"No," I answered, "this was far better."

"So why . . .?"

"Why? Because I like to see men together also, to perhaps watch then fucking as one sucks me."

"Would . . . would you like to see me with another man?" he asked.

"No, Kasra. I will keep you to myself," I replied, not because the image was not appealing, but because I knew he would do it if he thought it would please me, whether or not he wanted it for himself.

And then we slept. "Stay inside me as we sleep," he whispered as he drifted off, and I did.

I worried for a moment what would become of him, as he was so naive, and so eager to please and so willing. But I only worried for a moment. He was a man already and had to find his own way in the world and make his own mistakes.

Chapter Seven: Waylaid on the Road

Melioc rode up to the front of the caravan. He found Konan and reigned in his donkey, dismounted, and began walking beside the great barbarian, while leading his donkey by the reins. Behind them the caravan's camels were strung out in a single file, each connected to the one behind it by a rope and moving in their usual steady, rolling gait under the hot sun of the small, open plain they were crossing. On either side of them harsh, low hills rose up, but for a day it seemed the going was going to be easy on flat ground.

"What are your intentions?" the merchant blurted out after a long silence.

"About what?" the barbarian replied calmly, while continuing to walk along the narrow dirt road and scan the surrounding plain.

Melioc frowned. "About . . . him," he replied.

"Who?" Konan asked with a small smile on his lips.

"About, um, him." There was silence. "You know who I mean, Konan. Your boy. Young Kasra. He is in love with you, and the . . . the way you leave him and . . . and take your pleasure with other men . . . well, it hurts him greatly," Melioc finished in a rush, looking straight ahead.

"Ah. Kasra," Konan said, and a low rumble that was quiet laughter reached Melioc's ears.

"You laugh, Konan, but I have seen him. Seen him in distress and tears over it."

"Ah. Melioc." There was another rumble.

"So I ask you, what are your intentions regarding him?"

"My intention is to allow Kasra to accompany me to Persepolis, if he pleases me. And to offer him what protection I can until I am able to deliver him to his uncle. That is all I intend. And what, Melioc, would you have me intend?"

Melioc grunted and started to say something several times before finally saying, "He loves you. He is young, he is loyal and trusting, and—"

"Yes, Kasra is all those things, which is why he has need of me. And what is your interest in him, Melioc? I have seen how you watch him."

"My interest. My interest . . . ?" The merchant stopped in confusion, unable to go on for a few moments. "When I see him I am driven wild with lust. I admit it. I would have him if he would let me. I confess it. But he has eyes only for you and runs from me."

"Ah, and did you not try to take him when I was absent?" Konan said with a smile on his face.

Melioc gulped. "Yes. Yes I did. I could not help myself. He is a youth of such beauty, and such sweet nature, and innocence, I am lost. My desire for him eats at my entrails like a fire. It keeps me awake at night. I dream of him. Of his sweet smile of his gentle eyes, of his, of . . . of all of him. There is not a part of him that is not perfect. The gods gave him all the great asserts a youth can have, and that a poor man like me can long to be touched by. All of them. There—"

"Enough, Melioc. You are in love with him, far more than he is with me. But I will ask you this. What would you offer him? Each trip you make you take a new young lover with you, one who may stay in your favor for a few days or a moon or two, perhaps even for a whole journey. And then what? You find another young man who pleases you more at an inn along the way, or walking beside the road. And the old one is left behind, abandoned, or goes to make his bed with the camel drivers.

"Kasra will love whoever he is with, and whoever gives him pleasure and something to admire. He is too young to love more deeply yet. So tell me, Melioc, what would you give him if he loved you instead of me? You talk of him in tears when I am pleasuring my manhood inside other men. But what will happen to Kasra when you tire of him? Will he not shed tears then too?"

"I do not want him for myself," Melioc cried in anguish. "I only want to see you hurt him less." And with that he flung himself back into the saddle of his donkey, turned it about, and rode back, along the caravan, barking orders and abuse at anyone who caught his eye.

Then at the rear of the caravan he sighted Kasra, and he became silent and his eyes were suddenly full of longing.

* * * *

It had been thirteen days since Konan and Kasra had joined Melioc's caravan, and the journey to Persepolis was half done. After a day on the flat plain between the hills, they were climbing upward, into the mountains, where the road to Persepolis became a stony, narrow path weaving between low, dry hills covered with sparse vegetation. In the winter there was often snow upon the higher mountains and the pass was made treacherous by sudden extremes of weather. In summer the hills were baked hard with a searing sun, there was no water or shelter from the elements, and the heat alone made the road dangerous.

Now, it was spring and the weather was kind to the caravan, with warm dry days and cool nights when the men lay their blankets next to each other, about the small cooking fire, or beside their animals, and drank in the sight of a million stars above them before they slept.

The following morning they set off nervously as the climb that day was at its steepest and most treacherous. This was the part of the road where a merchant's camels sometimes slipped and fell to their knees under their burdens, and valuable loads could be lost down the steep slopes in the camels' clumsy attempts to regain their footing. If shouts and the whip would not raise the beast, the men would hurry to unload the unlucky animal so it could rise again and steady itself and the caravan could move along.

Late in the afternoon one of Melioc's camels fell so heavily it broke a leg and the men hurried about the screaming animal, cutting the rope that connected it fore and aft and removing its load. The caravan moved on by, while several men, including Kasra, held the camel steady, its keeper nursing the beasts head against his chest with tears in his eyes as his hands stroked it and his voice soothed it with soft words it had heard since it was young. When the other camels had passed by and moved on a way the keeper finally took his knife and cut the beast's throat, and the struggling animal's blood spouted from it as it screamed and died.

Kasra shook and tears sprung to his eyes also at the sound of the camel's screams. The whole caravan was restless, camels jerking unsteadily and braying in confusion, frightened by the noise and the smell of blood, their handlers struggling to control them. Kasra stayed as the dead beast's load was strapped to the back of one of the spare camels and he talked softly to the young beast, which as yet had no master of its own. When it rose up unsteadily under its burden, Kasra took its rope and led it to the rear of the caravan where it was tied between the last two camels.

Melioc had moved back and forth along the string of animals as the small drama unfolded and he dismounted by Kasra as the caravan moved off again.

"You did well, young man," he said, unable to stop himself embracing Kasra and with an unsteady voice he added, "few men are accepted so quickly by an animal as you were."

71

Kasra looked at his feet and up at the surrounding hills, anywhere but at the man who had tried to seduce him but a few days before, and he mumbled his polite thanks to Melioc's chest. But that night Kasra noticed Melioc going about the camp at sunset checking that the animals were secure and their loads were covered and handy and that all was well with the men, before retreating to the small tent that was all he had set up for himself at night now they were on the narrow mountain road.

Then Konan was there beside Kasra with a plate of hot food, holding it out to him.

Kasra took the plate with a smile, but once Konan was seated beside him, Kasra asked hesitantly, "What sort of man is Melioc?"

Konan considered the question before he replied. "Better than many, but not as good as some." He stopped then, thinking he had said it all, but saw Kasra was still looking at him, not eating and wanting more. "He treats his men with a light hand, unlike some, who use the whip freely on both men and beasts. He is honest and well liked and trusted. But he does not have the skill, or perhaps the wish, of become one of those wealthy traders in a fine warehouse. Now eat." Konan had no more to say, and Kasra bent to eating, using only his hand to bring the lumps of food to his mouth.

And even as Kasra ate Konan removed his weapons and lay them close by, ready if needed, and then removed his loincloth and lay upon the spread blanket and reached a hand for Kasra. He worked his fingers under the young man and buried one inside him as he reached his other hand to the young man's cock and balls, cupping them all in his great fist. Kasra groaned and put his plate aside, and their lips met in a kiss that was full of heat and passion, and neither was aware that Melioc had crept out of his tent and now hid nearby, unable to keep away.

Konan lifted himself up as Kasra slid beneath him and wrapped his legs about his hips, giving himself eagerly to the giant's kisses and reaching his hands to encircle and stroke the sword Konan had between his thighs. He wondered again at its great size and hardness and moaned at the thought of it soon entering his ass, which quivered at the touch of Konan's finger, which moved inside the tight but willing sheath into which he would soon plunge his great weapon. Kasra cried out as two fingers entered him, and writhed and arched his back, loving to feel Konan work him this way.

Later, as Konan worked his cock in and out of Kasra's channel, the young man turned his head and glimpsed Melioc watching them. He turned his eyes back to Konan but said nothing of what he had seen, and a part of him discovered he was excited by knowing they were being watched.

The following day the camels were restless, and loading them and getting them moving took longer than usual. The climb was no longer as steep, but they were entering a particularly narrow and winding section of road, and Konan went immediately to the front of the caravan and then moved off at a slow jog up the path ahead and out of sight around a bend.

Melioc quickly noticed Konan was gone and searched for Kasra, panicked that he too might have gone. "You are still here," he cried, when he found him, then recovered himself. "Do you know where Konan has gone?"

"He said he wanted to check the road ahead," Kasra replied, "the camels were behaving oddly when we loaded them, and he said it could mean more camels or donkeys are nearby."

"He is worried about trouble, is he? I think they just smell the dead beast form yesterday. This is a well-traveled road, patrolled regularly by the king's armies, and I have never been bothered by bandits on it before," he replied. But he went off and called his men to ready their weapons. And he sent a good reliable man, Darshan, off after Konan.

The atmosphere of the caravan became tense, and the beasts even more restless, making their handlers work hard to keep them on the narrow path and moving steadily. The men were worried and nervous, easily frightened and drawing their short, curved swords at any noise that came from the hills that now hemmed them in on all sides.

Melioc rode at the head of the caravan with three of his toughest men and was glad that Kasra was toward the rear, knowing it was the safest place for him to be if there was trouble. When neither Konan nor the man he had sent after him had returned after some time, he began to worry, fleetingly worrying if in taking the barbarian in, he had taken in a traitor. But he shook that thought off as unworthy of him and of the faith the trader Utana had placed in Konan.

Instead, he wondered if trouble waited ahead of them and if the two men had fallen to it.

He was so focused on seeking danger ahead that he didn't at first register the cries and shouts coming from behind him. He was a seasoned fighter, and once he heard them he knew them for the sounds of battle. "Kasra." He spoke the name under his breath, torn, wanting to rush back to help fight whoever was attacking them but knowing that an attack at the rear meant another was coming at the front.

But as the cries grew louder and the camels began to scream, he cried, "Stay here," to his three companions and turned his small horse and kicked it into a gallop, desperate to get to the rear of the caravan. He soon saw the fight ahead of him, the confusion of men between trying to move the heavily laden camels on and away from it. The frightened animals lurching and pulling to escape.

He rode on till he could see the men grouped at the rear fighting, sometimes hand to hand with white-robed men of the desert. By the time he joined the fight, the attackers were already trying to break away and run. And his arrival was enough to make them run off as fast as they could, scrabbling up the hills with several of his own men in pursuit.

"Leave them," Melioc cried. "See to the camels. Get them moving again," he ordered. Looking around frantically for Kasra. "Kasra? Where is Kasra?" he cried to the men around him, now seeing some wounded and bleeding, and several on the ground.

He slid from his horse, knelt by the first man on the ground, and turned him over to find him coming to. It was a man who had been with him for some years and had served him well. He moved on to the next man who was being helped up now by another.

"Can he walk?" he asked.

"No."

"Then put him on my horse," he ordered and hurried on to the next man, who lay beside a wounded camel. Another man was already there, turning the young man's head, and before he even reached them, Melioc saw Kasra's bloodied face.

Melioc was beside himself. Kasra seemed lifeless, and the blood was running down his forehead and off on to the ground.

"No, no," Melioc cried.

The merchant threw himself onto his knees beside the young man, and his arms embraced Kasra in one movement. Then he lifted him, pulling the young man's body to his chest and holding him there.

"No. No," Melioc moaned in anguish, his hands trying to feel if Kasra lived, and realizing he did as he bled and breathed still. Such a wave of relief flooded his body that he almost fainted, and he felt his manhood grow and harden to an aching size and firmness.

Melioc tried to recover himself then, as other man surrounded him and tried to lift Kasra from his arms. But he held on tight, unable to let go of the young man, even as he began to come around and moved. Then Konan was there, standing over them panting, with sweat running down his body.

"Where were you?" Melioc shouted angrily at him. "We were attacked, Kasra is hurt, and you were gone,"

"There were bandits ahead also," Konan replied, kneeling and wiping the blood form Kasra's forehead and shaking him gently.

"We took care of them, Konan and I, but were not able to do it fast enough to return before the rest of their band came at you from behind," Darshan, Melioc's own man who he had sent after Konan, said, and he was also panting and covered in sweat.

Kasra started to struggle to be free of Melioc's embrace, "I am all right," he stammered.

"We saw their camp and it looks to be full of booty. And slaves. There were two cages. And Donkeys," Darshan added excitedly.

Kasra pulled himself free of Melioc's arms and stood, shakily, and Konan placed an arm about his waist to help steady him. Melioc looked at Konan and Darshan.

"Where is their camp?" he asked.

"Ahead, not far," Darshan replied eagerly, knowing that if they rescued much booty from the bandit's camp, a share would pass to the men. Melioc was well known to be fair that way.

"You are all right?" Melioc asked Kasra, longing to be holding him still.

"Yes, yes," Kasra replied in embarrassment as everyone was standing about them now, and all, including Konan, could see how Melioc looked at him.

"Then we shall go and clear this camp, once we settle the beasts. Darshan, take four of the guards and go back there so the bandits don't get a chance to return and escape with the best of their plunder."

Darshan hurried off with four other men, as ordered.

"The rest of you," Melioc cried loudly, "see to the injured and settle the camels. There is work to do."

The men rushed off in excitement, their heads now full of visions of gold and loot, forgetting quickly how close some of them had come to death only minutes before. And Konan led Kasra away to a private spot where he could spread their blankets beside the road and Kasra could rest and his wound be cleaned and bound.

Chapter Eight: The Prisoner in the Cage

The bandit's camp was hidden between rough, rocky outcrops that screened it completely from anyone looking up toward it from the road, or down on it from the hill above.

"An ideal hiding place, and unusually large," Melioc said, "a good place to rest for the night, or even a day, if the weather is bad. We will rest here tonight ourselves," he added enthusiastically.

There were half a dozen donkeys standing about, a small enclosed cart, a cage on wheels, various bundles, and sacks, some with their contents spilling out of them. This told Melioc and his men that some of the bandits had probably made it back there and taken with them what was most valuable and easiest to carry. A trail of small bronze icons, perhaps leaking from a hastily filled sack, led up the hill.

"Do not follow it," shouted Melioc, when one of the guards started to follow the trail, "It may be a trap. We will follow it later when more men are here to guard our backs."

The guard hurriedly returned, and they continued to inspect and repack the scattered goods and to sort through what was in the sacks and bundles and arrange it all neatly. Meanwhile, others captured and tethered the donkeys, and they looked briefly at what was in the cart but were wary of touching it. The cage on wheels was empty, it's door broken half off.

Kasra, clean and bandaged, arrived not long after with Konan, and they brought more men. Konan immediately looked at the cart on wheels, "They are gone," he said.

"Who?"

"The two youths who were locked in that cage, but the cart still has its occupant." And he led Melioc to the small enclosed cart, saying, "Have you seen her?"

"Who?" asked Melioc in surprise. looking in.

It was a small cart suitable for a donkey to pull, but most of its sides were wooden rails so that it was completely enclosed, and inside in one corner was a pile of ragged black clothing.

Konan unchained the small door that was at the rear of the cart and leaning inside grasped the rags and pulled. The bundle immediately erupted into a thrashing, screaming monster, biting and kicking at Konan as he dragged it out and stood it on the ground in front of a stunned Melioc.

"What is it?"

Konan tore off some of the fabric and a face appeared, and it was apparent that the face was female and also that her hands and ankles were tied.

"I think it's female," Konan said, smiling.

Kasra had appeared beside him and stood open mouthed. "A woman? But why, why is she in a cage? Is she mad?"

"No, I'd say she is a prisoner, held for ransom most likely, or else she is a well-trained virgin being taken to the slave markets untouched."

Kasra gasped. "But she is so young. She's not much more than a girl!"

The girl indeed did look barely eighteen and looked at Kasra and then spat at him, but he seemed to hardly even notice.

"Who are you?" Melioc asked her in a gentle voice, but she stayed stubbornly silent though he tried many languages. "Well, we will have to keep her caged until we find out who she is and what her value was," he said, when he had given up trying to get anything out of her.

"Her value?" Kasra asked, "How can you keep her in a cage and worry about her value as if she were . . . were a bag of wheat?"

"She is caged for a reason Kasra, most probably to ensure she keeps her virginity while surrounded by lonely men. Whoever she is, she will be worth less without that still intact," Konan told him as he pushed the girl back inside the cart and rechained the door.

"Oh," Kasra said, thinking. "It's still not right for a young woman to be imprisoned like that," he mumbled as he looked at her.

"You may bring her food," Konan said, "and will be responsible for ensuring her cage stays secure and that she is safe till we reach Persepolis."

"But . . ." Melioc started to protest.

"Kasra has much to learn of women, Melioc, and he is honest and reliable," the barbarian said as if that explained it all. "If anyone touches her, it will be on your head, Kasra," he added looking at the young man seriously.

Kasra nodded his head just as seriously. "I will not fail you, Konan, or . . . or Melioc," he added shyly.

"Are you hungry?" Kasra then asked the young woman in a gentle voice, as if talking to a child.

She spat at him again, but as before he seemed to not notice it. "I will bring you food anyway," he said and trotted off back to the caravan.

"These raiders were dressed as if they were desert men, but their saddles and other things in this camp are the work of Medes, not Persians or desert tribesmen," Melioc said as he and Konan walked away.

"Yes," said Konan, frowning, "so they were."

* * * *

"Konan, what do you know of women?" Kasra asked several nights later, as he lay spooned against the barbarian with the barbarians tumescent manhood buried deep inside his passage.

Konan laughed. "Very little but that it's best to avoid them."

"Almira . . . I call her Almira, she has no gratitude for what I do for her. None at all."

"Ah," was all Konan could reply without laughing.

"What . . .what is lying with a woman like?"

"You will have to find that out for yourself Kasra. I cannot tell you. Remember it is your duty to protect Almira till we reach Persepolis, and you must not lie with her."

* * * *

The rest of the caravan's journey to Persepolis was uneventful. Kasra cared for Almira as well as he could, taking her food and water at least three times a day, often missing time for his own midday meal to carry food to her. And Konan watched him more carefully than Kasra realized.

Kasra sobbed and hid from Melioc one evening when Konan went to the two camel drivers who he had shared time with once before. And Melioc pined and stroked himself each night he watched Konan fuck Kasra mightily. He was sure that Kasra had on at least one occasion clearly seen him watching their joining and wondered what the youth's silence about it meant.

And the other men who worked on the caravan were generally occupied with their own wondrous dreams of what they would do with their shares of the bandit's valuable loot when they reached the great new capital city of the Persian empire, Persepolis.

Soon the city walls came in sight and the excitement of the end of a journey descended on them all, even the great barbarian, and he took out the clay seals he had in his pouch and examined them—Utana's seal, the seal of the Mede, Vivana, and the third seal, the most important one he had been entrusted with by Vivana, and which had brought him to Persepolis with a greater purpose than idle curiosity and finding an easy road to follow to the east.

And that night as he lay with Kasra, he said, "Tomorrow I shall deliver you to your uncle, and our time together will be over."

Kasra lay against him, half of him wanting to sob like a child at the thought of losing Konan, his lover, and the other half filled with excited anticipation for his new life in a great city.

"I will become a great man here," Kasra said. "My Uncle is wealthy and will find a place for me within his business, or perhaps even at the court of the king. Then when I am a man of substance I will find myself a beautiful wife of good family and start my own family," he said, stopping himself from thinking of losing Konan.

"Noble dreams," Konan replied, kissing his lover's neck and feeling the pleasure of Kasra's willing and exuberant passion for what he knew must be the last time.

"And you . . . where do you go?" Kasra asked.

"I have business here and then I continue my journey to the east, back to where I came from. And when I arrive there I will wait for another to arrive, if he is not already there."

Kasra felt a surge of jealousy, "Who? Who do you go to?"

"Someone I once knew," The barbarian replied, "but it will be many years before I arrive there."

"Is it far?"

"Very far. Across the seas and up into the mountains to the north of the port of Tyrins."

Kasra embraced him and they kissed, Kasra's body crying out for the now so familiar ecstasy that his lover gave him each time he worked his great manhood inside him. His legs wrapped about the barbarian's hips and the giant set him in his lap with their two cocks brushing against each other as their lips and hands explored the other's body. Then when they were ready, Konan lifted Kasra up and guided his great pole to the young man's hole and settled him down on it.

81

Slowly. But even slowly Kasra gasped and moaned at the feel of it. Slowly he descended, wondering if he would ever fully take it. And then finding his ass resting against Konan's golden bush, the barbarian's great sword moving inside him, gliding, digging, touching him everywhere, filling him, giving him waves of pleasure. Which he was sure no other man could ever give him.

The barbarian drove in and out of Kasra and made magic love to his channel in various positions for most of the night, so that when dawn came, Kasra was swimming in a sea of the giant's seed and unable to feel anything but mellow and totally satiated.

That morning the caravan seemed to Kasra to move faster, as if rushing to its destination knowing it would bring them to a new world, to what everyone desired most.

For one among them though, that was far from true. Melioc glanced often at Kasra, feeling his belly knot up at the thought of never seeing the youth again, and he was rough and short tempered with his men. Though with their heads full of thoughts of loot to spend and the great city ahead, his men easily ignored his mood.

And soon Kasra himself felt a strange confusion building up and whirling about inside him. Almira had fascinated him since the first moment he saw her face, but after all his care for her, she had tried to escape that morning. He had been feeding her thin slices of grilled camel meat, which he'd had to beg the cook for, when she had kicked him hard in his balls, and jumped out of the cage door and past him. He'd only just caught her and had to fight her to get her back in the cage, and while they struggled she'd bitten him and screeched vicious things that shocked him. He was still aching and sore, from both Konan's riding of him and her kick, and was becoming disillusioned about her, having imagined before that she was gentle and had been badly treated. Now he wondered why he had spent so much time looking after her but knew there was still something about her that drew him.

Even after she attacked him, he'd tried to help her. "We will be there soon, in Persepolis. Tell Melioc who you are, and he will do what is right. He is a good man. Why won't you tell him who you are? I can see you are from a good family." It was obvious from the way she ate that she was well brought up. "If you won't tell Melioc, then tell me, and I will go to your family secretly and tell them where you are," he begged her. But all she had done was spit at him. At which point he'd suddenly started to see her as an evil tormentor, rather than a sweet young woman such as he might one day marry.

Almost as soon as the caravan began moving in the morning they had got a first distant glimpse of the palaces raised up on the platform that was Persepolis, but it was not till noon that they had arrived at the outskirts of the rapidly growing town that on three sides surrounded the raised platform backing onto the hill, which was where the king's palaces and government buildings of Persepolis stood, with more magnificent palaces being built.

Melioc immediately led his caravan to an area by the markets, where they began to unload the beasts before they were led away, out of the city and into a field of good grass, which they could feed on for the next few days. The donkeys and Melioc's two horses were put into a stable and fed and watered.

Kasra made himself busy helping the men with the work, but too soon, it seemed, Konan came and said, "It's time to find your uncle. Come."

They stopped to tell Melioc they were leaving, "I go now to find my uncle," Kasra told him, suddenly wishing he weren't leaving the caravan.

"What, already? But . . . but there is unloading still," Melioc said, wanting to hold him there, but also realizing he couldn't. "And . . .and, Kasra, you know you are welcome to return. More than welcome," Melioc stammered, not knowing anything else he could say, unable to stop him going and finally nodding his head several times and turning away, unable to say more.

Konan asked directions to the house of Amahl of Gasterjean, the official, and they were directed toward a street in the inner city just below the raised platform on which the palaces stood. They arrived at the fine large house with a statue of a horse at its gate as they had been told and found its courtyard gates were standing open. As Konan entered Kasra held back, suddenly nervous at meeting a man he had not seen since he was a small child, and one, he also suddenly remembered, his father had not been known to say much good of. Kasra finally went to follow Konan, but the barbarian stepped back sharply and almost knocked him over.

"We had best check that this really is your uncle's house," Konan whispered, after pushing Kasra against the wall beside the gate, then pulling him along quickly, up the paved street.

"But . . .but we followed the directions, it's—"

"Shhh," Konan hissed, and pulled Kasra past several large houses before entering another open gate into another courtyard, where they could see an elderly man sitting beneath a tree.

"Greetings, friend," Konan said, bowing politely to the old man. "We are visitors to this great city. The house with the small horse statue at its gate, is that the house of the official, Amahl of Gasterjean?"

"Official? Yes, I suppose so, his name is Amahl, and he is from Gasterjean, I have heard. Though he is seldom at court nowadays. He has fallen from favor, and it's not surprising. Why do you ask?"

"I was recommended to do some business with him, but I am not sure if he is reliable. There were . . . visitors in his courtyard whom I have met elsewhere."

"If you want to sell him the young man, you'd be better going to old Pharos. He will give you a more honest price for him."

Kasra gasped, and Konan hurried on. "What business does Amahl mainly do from home now?"

"He mostly lends. Taking the families' lands when they can't repay him. But then, only fools borrow from one like him."

"Thank you, friend. Unfortunately, I have been obliged to visit him on a friend's behalf. There are three young men in his courtyard I am sure I have met before in another town, and who I think are dishonest, and I was very surprised to see them there."

"Three young men? Ha, the ones there now? Three young thieves more like. Every few months they come to borrow money from him," the man said, winking. "Surprising how much jewelry they seem to have come by in their travels and can give him as surety."

"Yes. It is," Konan said. "Do you know when Amahl will return? I had planned to be here only a short time."

"I heard he has gone to the palace, so I doubt he will return till midafternoon. Not long after he left his servants took advantage of his absence to go out visiting themselves, which signifies a long absence."

"Thank you for your help. I wish you and your family good health," Konan said politely.

"Come Kasra." Konan pulled the young man back into the roadway and stopped. "What do you know of your uncle?"

Kasra shrugged. "Very little but that he is an official, and rich and made his fortune here. What is—"

"The three young men who took you from the ferry are waiting in the courtyard of your uncle's house, and as our friend said, they have been here before."

Kasra gaped at Konan for a few minutes. "The three men? Those men? With braided hair and bracelets and arm bands of gold?"

"Yes, those three."

"But . . ." Kasra was taking a moment to adjust to the new situation. "I will get my gold back," he suddenly cried; darting off up the road, back to his uncle's house.

"No, no," cried Konan grabbing him. "You are no match for them." he added looking at Kasra and thinking. Then he pulled Kasra close and whispered in his ear.

"But . . ." Kasra started to protest.

"You will do as I say, or I doubt you will see your gold again."

"But . . ."

"Will you do as I say, Kasra?"

Kasra stood there, obviously torn; his face flushed with anger and frustration, until his body suddenly drooped in resignation. "Yes. Yes . . . all right. You are right, I am no match for them alone. And my uncle. . . .well . . . my father never said much good about him. I knew he was wealthy though and did not think he could be such a wicked man as he seems to be, but perhaps he does not know what these three are, perhaps they have fooled him also with their fine hair and clothing."

Chapter Nine: An Unexpected Meeting

I was itchy and in a bad mood. Darius and Perviz were also. And I was horny but doubted they were, as they were rarely as horny as me, so saw no relief coming to me from them.

We sat on two wooden benches under the big olive tree in the courtyard of Amahl's house, and Darius was again complaining that it was Amahl's fault that we'd had to share a flea-ridden bed in a dump of an inn for the last two nights, and hadn't even had enough coin to use the public baths the previous afternoon. There had been no money for wine the previous night either, which Perviz hadn't stopped moaning about. And I was hungry. More annoyed at the rumble in my empty belly than anything else.

I was getting tired of the bickering and starting to wonder if it was time I wandered off to see what I could steal by way of food, and if there might be a fine man about to fuck me, when the barbarian entered the courtyard.

"Look who's here!" I hissed, elbowing Darius, who sat beside me, in the ribs.

Darius stopped complaining and looked at the new arrivals, "Where have we seen the barbarian giant before? He looks familiar."

"He'd be hard to forget," I replied, knowing I certainly hadn't, and feeling the ache in my crotch increasing, "he's the barbarian from the river crossing we waited at a moon ago, where we met that youth we took to Xerxes."

"Ah, yes. He looks well fed, and even has a servant now. I wonder if—"

"Hail friends, we meet again," the barbarian greeted us as he approached, followed by his hooded and cowering, dirty, straggly haired, serving man, who was dressed in ragged clothing and carrying a large wineskin and a sack.

Darius jumped up, "Hail, friend. What brings you here? We have met before, but not spoken as we were all occupied with our own business at the time. Here, you and your servant are welcome. Come, take a seat," he said, indicating the bench next to me and moving to the one opposite and sitting next to Perviz.

"My thanks, but the youth you call my servant will sit away from us, as he smells of camels," the barbarian replied, taking a seat himself.

The young servant, I assumed he was young, but covered in dirt and hooded with his hair hanging in rat's tails over his face, it was hard to tell. His clothes were ragged and he indeed did smell strongly of something, which may have been camels, so I was glad he did not sit next to us. Instead, he shuffled away and sat down on the dirt in a shady spot close by.

"Do you have business with the official, Amahl, also?" the barbarian asked us.

"Yes, but tell us of your journey," Darius said diplomatically, as one never knew what Amahl's visitors might be there for. "And forgive my manners. I am Darius, and these two companions of mine are Perviz and Ashkan."

"Greetings. I am Konan," the barbarian replied, "I am here to see Amahl on a friend's account. Is he not at home?"

The man before me was truly a magnificent barbarian, but, unfortunately, he couldn't be the legendary Konan. That man, I was sure, was a myth, or long dead if he had ever lived.

"No, he was called away urgently, to the palace, and bade us wait his return," Darius replied smoothly. "So we wait, as if we leave he is bound to return straight after, and we leave the city tomorrow. When our business in Persepolis is done, we take the road to Ur."

"Ur. A wondrous city, I have heard," the barbarian replied. "Well, I too will wait, at least for a while. I have wine," he added. "Shall we drink to pass the time?"

I have never seen Perviz become a man's good friend so quickly as he became the barbarian's. And when the barbarian summoned his servant to bring the wineskin to him, he drank from it then passed it first to Perviz, who clung to his side now like a pet dog. I think Perviz would have drunk the skin dry if he could have. He certainly drank from the skin long enough for Darius to have to pull it from him for his turn. I was last to drink.

The wine was good. Very good. And being hungry and horny, I drank more than I normally would have.

"I want to find out a price for this youth. My friend acquired him along the road, but is now tired of him. He was told that Amahl could advise a price."

Darius looked at the youth as if assessing him. "Yes, Amahl will surely advise you when he returns. He has some experience dealing in young men."

"Yes, stay, Amahl will know exactly what he is worth. He will give a good price for him," Perviz added, keen to keep the barbarian's wine skin there.

We were all quickly becoming quite happy on its contents, and I, not having been well fucked for several days and already horny when he arrived, was now highly aroused by the closeness of such a muscular and well-built man.

"Last time I saw you, you were befriending a fine-looking youth from the country," the barbarian said. "I had been interested in him myself and disappointed that you made off with him first. He was a fine, tall young man, with lean, but well-muscled limbs and a firm-looking ass. I have wondered on several occasions how well you enjoyed yourselves with him."

Darius smiled, relieved I am sure at the change of subject away from Amahl. Amahl was a man of shady dealings, who was becoming known as such around Persepolis. Once he had been a man of some reputation and standing but now . . . now he was wealthier, but people tended to avoid those they knew did business with him. Which on this trip had not been helpful for us in our business.

"Ah yes, a fine young virgin. He was well ridden," I replied, and memories of that night only increased my arousal.

"Ah, tell me more," the barbarian said, turning to me and passing me the wine skin.

I drank while my mind tried to form an arousing story for him. And I noticed that his hand had strayed to rest on my thigh, and that there was something large growing beneath his loin cloth. My own manhood lurched at the sight of that, coupled with the feel of his big hand firmly gripping my leg.

"We took him to a friend's house for the night, and there a very beautiful young man made free with his ass as his older lover looked on. The man was also a visitor there, and our young friend had quickly taken a great fancy to him," I explained. Memories of that young god fingering our young friend's ass and finding him to already be full of another man's seed came vividly to mind, setting my pole to growing even harder.

"And how was his first taking? Was he well prepared? Did he cry out?"

"He was kissing the stranger and moaning deeply, eager to feel him enter him," I said, now panting slightly, feeling the barbarian's hand at the top of my thigh and the back of his fingers pressing against my now-engorged organ and encouraging the further parting of my thighs. I wanted that hand wrapped about me, and I wanted more. The good wine and my horniness were combining.

"First his ass was oiled and well fingered," I said wanting the barbarian's own thick fingers digging inside my entrance, and moaned unexpectedly as his hand moved to cup and squeeze my manhood.

"They kissed," I stammered, "like this," I added turning my head and leaning my face closer to the barbarian's. His mouth met mine, and I opened my lips to his probing tongue, as my hand searched for his huge organ and grasped it. I gasped when I found it; it was so thick and long.

Perviz suddenly noticed that the provider of the fine wine we were drinking was interested in something other than his chatter and quickly fell to his knees between the barbarian's spread thighs and pulled the huge pole from my hand and began to cover it with his lips. The barbarian broke our kiss at this point, but I wanted his attention back on me, not on Perviz, and reached down for the giant's balls and cupped and squeezed them. The barbarian moaned, and his hand tugged at me through my robes. I quickly pulled them off so I was sitting there naked but for my sandals, my gold bracelets, and my earrings. The barbarian worked my now-throbbing pole with his great hand and resumed our kiss, and I quickly spouted my seed for him.

Now I wanted more and stood, but before I could do anything, he grabbed me by the waist and lifted me and set me down so I now straddled the bench with my ass toward him and he pushed me forward so I lay on the timber before him. I reached back and parted my own cheeks with my hands, wanting him to see my twitching hole there before him. I moaned in fear of the size of him, but it was a desperately wanting fear.

He pushed a finger into my entrance, and I moaned my eager anticipation of what was to come.

"I will enjoy this far more than Perviz's mouth," he said in a deep, husky voice.

The barbarian then straddled the bench behind me, and Perviz moved with him, still working only the first half of that mighty weapon with his lips and tongue, unable to get more inside him. But I was sure that if I was prepared my ass would take it all.

"Oil," the barbarian demanded loudly, and his servant came running over.

* * * *

The only time I had seen other men together before that afternoon, well that I could remember anyway, was seeing Konan with the merchant the night before he first took me. Now I was soon hard, and hardly able to stop from stroking myself as I sat on the dirt under the olive tree, pretending to be a filthy downtrodden servant, and watched the two young men begin to work on Konan and he on them.

When Konan called for the oil pot, I dug it out of the sack beside me and struggled up and ran it over to him. Standing closer to them, I could clearly see exactly what was happening, with the young thief, Ashkan, spreading his cheeks and exposing his hole immediately before Konan and me and the head of the other man, Perviz, bobbing up and down on Konan's engorged weapon. I was familiar with every vein and crease of that great tool, but had never seen Konan drive it into another man. I admit I was so aroused that I was leaking juice from my own cock, and on the point of spouting my seed fully.

I stood there with the oil pot in my shaking hand, watching as Konan placed a thumb at each side of the hole of the young many lying belly down before him, and pulled it open.

"Pour," he ordered in a husky voice, and I took a moment to understand what he meant, but then I poured the oil over the spread entrance.

A surprising amount of oil seemed to disappear inside that hole, while more ran over Konan's fingers and down the young thief's crease, and I was quivering with arousal, wanting it to be my asshole being prepared for Konan to fuck. But also I felt an urge I had never felt before, the urge to drive my own throbbing pole into that hole. To drive and drive and . . . I felt my seed rise and found I was gripping myself and unable to stop moving my hand. I spouted my release beneath my robe.

Konan let me stay and watch as he plunged two thick oily fingers into Ashkan's hole. What a sight. One that had my own asshole twitching at the memory of how it felt when Konan did the same to me. He moved his fingers about then to the moans and whimpers of the young man lying belly down on the bench. Then Konan ordered me away and I hurried to sit on the ground again, but with my hand wrapped about my own organ now, which was soon throbbing yet again, demanding the release I could now stroke it to, as I watched Konan open Ashkan's ass further.

Darius was seated on the bench opposite them, watching with slitted eyes and a slack mouth and had pulled up his robe and had his own rod in one hand, as the other roamed his body. Then he got up and moved to straddle the bench in front of the prone Ashkan and pressed the end of his cock at his friend's lips, which parted eagerly, and soon the young man had both his ass and his mouth full.

I spouted my cream into my robe again, but hardly went soft I was so on fire from what I was watching.

Konan now pushed Perviz off his weapon and guided it to the well-oiled hole before him, where one thumb still pulled it open. Pervis, eager to help, reached his hand over and pulled the hole wider as Konan pressed the great head of his cock to it. I couldn't actually see what was happening, but from Konan's movements, I was sure that it resisted at first, then gave suddenly and allowed him entrance, but only a short way. Ashkan's prone body arched and he raised his hips and widened his legs, obviously being sorely tested by what was trying to drive into his channel. I knew well the feel of that great organ entering my ass, and my rim twitched and clenched and opened at the memory of it, while I was stroking myself and panting as I watched Konan move in deeper and begin to pump in and out.

Thoughts of Melioc briefly came to me, and of how, at night, on the road to Persepolis, he had often hidden nearby and watched Konan pump in and out of my ass, while the merchant stroked himself. And I came again.

Perviz was now sprawled on the ground by the bench taking long drinks from the wine skin and stroking himself to his own completion. But then Darius pulled his organ from Ashkan's mouth and stood up with his engorged rod in his hand and quickly had Perviz on his hands and knees and was fucking him doggy fashion, pounding his ass wildly before jerking and falling across his back.

My eyes moved back to Konan, who now crouched above the bench, gripping Ashkan's hips, lifting them off the bench with Ashkan's shaking legs dangling down as my lover pumped into his ass. The young thief came yet gain and Konan pulled out, his cock still hard and throbbing, and moved to Darius, who lay collapsed over Pervis. Darius tried to scramble away but failed, and Konan barely prepared him before he plunged his weapon deep inside him to screams and wails, stifled quickly by Konan's hand across his mouth.

Perviz lay where he was on the ground beneath them and seemed to have passed out, not surprising considering how much wine he had drunk. Ashkan had the wine skin now and was drinking from it as he looked on at Konan fucking Darius.

"I am a far better bottom than Darius," Ashkan cried.

"Tell me more of the young man you took away," Konan said in a rough voice.

"Him. Him . . . .it was a disaster. Xerxes thought he was smart but was a fool, and we had to leave in a hurry." Ashkan was starting to slur his words and leaned over on the bench as if he were falling down on it. "He wanted us to get rid of him, of . . . of Kasra, but Darius wouldn't kill him, so we just left him in a ditch . . . to live or die. . . . But to see him with that young god was . . . .ahhhhh sooooo gooood . . ." Ashkan said as he fell sideways on the bench and passed out.

Konan pulled out of Darius's ass, and Darius also fell to the ground. Then Konan tuned to me with his throbbing pole in his hand, "So, they are wicked men, but not as evil as many, and you wanted to know what it might be like to lie with a woman," he said looking at me with slitted eyes and a loose smile. "Well, I think you may also want to know what it is to lie with a man, so let me see you enter Ashkan."

I was looking at Konan's throbbing pole and more interested in having that inside me than in discovering anything, but he rearranged the young thief who was almost conscious again and eager to be fucked on the bench, and directed me to sit behind Ashkan and spread the young thief's cheeks and exposed his hole. I gulped as I saw the oil and cream leaking out of it and tentatively held the head of my own throbbing organ to it and pushed. It seemed to slide in like a knife into its well-worn sheath, and I bottomed quickly. I sighed, and I wondered at the feeling of the embrace of Ashkan's passage. The young man moaned, not as unconscious as I had imagined. I quivered in a sort of fear, then at Konan's urging began to plow the thief's ass.

I was enjoying that greatly when Konan moved onto the bench behind me, and I turned my head and we kissed before he pushed me forward over Ashkan's back and fed oiled, thick fingers into my eager and twitching asshole. Then it was his cock at my entrance and the pain of it's first entrance before the pleasure came, and soon he was moving in and out of me as I was moving in the passage of Ashkan and moaning and whimpering in the overwhelming fullness and completeness of it and losing myself totally in the taking.

When Konan filled me with his cream, and I had filled Ashkan, we moved apart, and I saw my juice dribble from the hole before me as I withdrew, and shivered as I felt Konan's cream run from my own ass.

"Collect their gold," he ordered me then, and I slowly did so, stripping the bracelets, earrings, and armbands from the three young thieves while they slept soundly, overcome by the drugged wine we had brought them.

We left them alive, though, as they had been generous enough to leave me alive.

"What now?" Konan asked me then.

I could think of nothing but to leave my uncle's house and return to Melioc's caravan. When we arrived at the familiar camp with its familiar faces and smells, it felt like coming home.

Konan and Melioc went off into Melioc's tent and I hurried to see Almira, finding her still in her cage, huddled in a corner.

I begged her to tell me what her family were like and if she wanted to see them again, or needed to escape from them, now wondering if her family were as bad as my uncle had turned out to be. She only spat at me. I begged her again to tell me who her family were so I could let them know where she was. She hissed rude things at me, and I left wondering why I bothered with her.

Chapter Ten: Finding a Lover

"Kasra's uncle is a thief in his own right. We arrived at his house to find the three young men who had abused Kasra and left him for dead were waiting for his uncle, Amahl. Apparently they regularly did business with him," Konan said once he and Melioc were seated inside Melioc's tent.

Melioc was horrified, "But, how . . .what . . . ?"

"They have been taught a lesson," Konan replied, smiling, "and Kasra has a small amount of gold back from them. But now it's time I completed the other business I have here in Persepolis. So, as a friend, Melioc, I tell you now that I must gain an audience with the king's first adviser. Give me what advice you can as to how I may do this."

"Ah. You aim high, friend. But I can introduce you to him," Melioc replied. "I have brought other loads of fine materials, oils, and spices here for the palace and have met him before."

And to aid Konan, Melioc sent a man to the palace to make an appointment in his name with the first adviser, and the messenger quickly returned with a time for the following day.

* * * *

I had made myself useful about the camp, having no idea if I should now return to my father's farm and go back to my old life or take some other path. My fine plans of making a life in Persepolis lay in ruins; my foolish dreams were proved to be no more than that—foolish, youthful dreams.

When Melioc and Konan emerged from Melioc's tent, the merchant moved about the camp checking on his goods and the tents, but I felt his eyes on me and felt that he watched me whenever he could. I looked at him also, and I admit I was aroused now by knowing that he had watched Konan and me together so many times. But each time our eyes met I hurriedly looked away again and he soon retuned to his tent. I knew that Konan would soon be gone, and I had accepted that, but Melioc was still here, and his caravan was the place I now felt most at home in.

"Tomorrow I shall begin my own business in Persepolis, and we shall visit the king's palace. And when that business is done I leave. So, we spend another night or two here together," Konan said when he joined me. And he smiled that sort of smile at me that made my manhood stiffen and lurch.

"Another two nights?" I sighed with anticipation.

I was nervous and highly strung at the sight of him. I may have lost my virginity a moon before, but that day I had lost my innocence and become much more of a man. And now I wanted to discover all that the great barbarian could show me before I said good-bye to him forever. For I knew he would not take me with him and our parting would be the last I saw of him. Though I was sure I would hear more of him and of his adventures, for I had found now that he was a famous man and many were in awe of him. Yet, for a moon I had lain with him ignorant of his fame.

Suddenly Konan grabbed me, laughing at my surprise, and swinging me about, he tossed me over his shoulder and carried me off to Melioc's tent. Once inside he dropped me among a pile of cushions on thick rugs only a couple of arm's lengths from where Melioc already sat. The merchant looked at us in obvious surprise, and his mouth fell open when Konan dropped his loincloth and began to stroke his already stiff manhood to hardness. I lay among the cushions, pleased that Konan was already hard for me, but in confusion— watching him, aroused as always by the sight of his manhood growing steadily longer and harder in preparation for taking possession of me—as I was also burning in embarrassment at having Melioc there. I attempted to rise and leave, but Konan placed a foot on my chest and pushed me back down.

My own manhood was aching, I admit. I was confused. Aroused by Konan before me and the memory of the earlier wild takings—watching Konan as he took the young thieves in Amahl's courtyard. And I found my hand was moving up and down my own organ as I looked up, seeing Konan's great balls hanging above me, between his parted thighs, and his hand stroking his great pole.

My breathing was rough and panting, and I tried not to look at Melioc.

Then Konan bent and ripped off my plain short robe as if he were taking me roughly for the first time. But we were not alone, and, aroused as I was, I still tried to cover myself. Konan only smiled and, lifting my hips, twisted me about and stuffed cushions under my lower back, raising my ass up high. I was all confusion and burning at knowing that my ass was now pointed directly at Melioc as Konan moved and knelt above my head, looking toward my raised ass and presenting his cock head to my lips. I opened up and sucked on him as I had learned, while he moved his mouth to my entrance.

Oh, that tongue! It was able to enter me and did things inside me few men can do with their stiff organs. But I had been aroused by, and welcomed, everything Konan had worked inside my passage: his fingers, his cock, even the round-ended smooth wooden thing he had brought and used on me one night when a party with other men had tired him out. Yes, even that, when he worked it into me and moved it inside my channel as he sucked on my hard nipples, had sent waves of ecstasy through my body.

Now I moaned, my head full of wonder at what Melioc thought of me now that he was there below my ass, knowing he could see Konan's tongue moving in out of my quivering hole.

Then Konan moved his head and took my cock into his mouth—and then my balls—and rolled and sucked on them as I moaned and whimpered. I felt him push my thighs apart and run a finger to my hole, and I arched and cried out and spouted my cream into his throat, for I knew that Melioc saw Konan's finger entering me. And the memory of that sight as I had seen it when Konan's fingers entered Ashkan's hole in the courtyard of Amahl's house, overwhelmed me.

Suddenly I had difficulty making myself suck on Konan's huge pole as I felt movement at my ass and felt another of Konan's fingers enter me. I quivered and moaned. Then it was three fingers and then something thicker than a finger, but I barely wondered what it was. If I hadn't just spouted my load, I would have spouted then though at the stretching feel of it.

Then I felt something else at my ass, and Konan moved back and squatted behind my head and his hands went to running up and down my body, but still I felt my ass filled. I looked up, confused, to see Melioc pumping his good-sized organ in and out of my hole, a look of pure ecstasy on his face as he gazed down at me. I felt my body tighten, understanding that look, and I spouted what little cream I had left up my belly.

Too soon Melioc filled me with his seed and fell upon me and we kissed. I pulled him to me, knowing that the caravan was more my home now than anywhere else was ever likely to be. I felt Konan move and glanced over Melioc's shoulder as the giant moved behind him and knelt. For a moment I quivered fearfully at the thought he might enter me with Melioc still buried inside me, but no, he grasped Melioc's hips and began to prepare him. The merchant made to get up and push him off, but I pulled him to me and kissed his mouth and wrapped my legs about his waist and gripped him tight. Konan prepared the merchant's ass and entered him gently to his groans and whimpers. I held him to me and kissed his face and neck until our lips met in a long kiss, where he possessed my mouth completely, as Konan possessed his ass.

I could feel the movement of Melioc inside me and feel him growing, his body driven by the pumping of Konan inside his channel, and I lost myself in the heat of it.

At some time Konan fell across Melioc's back and kissed me, and the next thing I remember was realizing that he was gone. For a moment I wanted to run after him and call him back, but then I recovered myself and realized that the next day we would all go to the palace together, so he had to return.

"I am not usually so wild, Kasra," Melioc said to me, as he eased himself into a more comfortable lying position with me cupped into his body.

"And but a moon ago I was an innocent virgin," I replied, happy to lie there with Melioc's tumescent organ resting inside my channel.

Chapter Eleven:
Forebodings for the Future

I left Melioc and Kasra locked together in the tent and, entering the city of Persepolis, walked to the stone-flagged earthen platform on which the king's great palaces and temples stood.

A broad flight of steps led up to the great platform, and on each side of it were stone walls where the figures of ambassadors bringing tribute to the Persian king and of captives being led into slavery were carved. In the light of early evening the figures seemed almost alive, and as men and women still hurried up and down the steps on business, the sounds of feet on stone added to the power of the images.

It must have been a wondrous sight, I thought, to see that place on a day of ceremony or celebration, when hundreds, if not thousands moved up and down those steps in processions.

At the top of the stairs I paused to look about and saw the great wonder and size of the buildings, then wandered outside the hall of the hundred columns, then the palace of King Darius and the older palace of King Xerxes. Then suddenly a voice hailed me and I turned to see a Persian giant approaching.

He was a magnificent figure of a man. One who made my breath catch in my throat. A dark-haired Persian in the finest, yet plainest, of linen robes with his black hair braided and oiled and hanging almost to his waist. His fine beard was also braided, but there was no gold among any of the braids. But gold was at his neck, and he wore a sword belt with a gold trimmed sword in it as well as a knife and other items, and in one hand he carried a shield, small and decorative, but also functional, and in the other was held a lance, ebony shafted and iron tipped; that stood even taller than him.

We both stopped for a moment at seeing each other. Then we both moved slowly toward each other.

"Greetings, stranger," I called to him as we drew nearer. "I am Konan the barbarian."

"Ah," he sighed with a smile. "So you are not a story told by imaginative fools after all. And I am Mardinaya, leader of the king's own bodyguard."

"So you are no imaginary legend either, Mardinaya," I said with surprise. For I had heard of an immortal giant called Mardinaya who served the Persian king. But when men described him as bigger and more well endowed than I, I confess I had doubted them. I had never seen a man who came close to me in size, except among the mountain tribes.

Mardinaya ran his gaze up and down my body with a smile on his lips and his eyes wide, and I did the same to him, sorry my view was spoiled by his fine, long linen robe. But knowing too that he was a man, such as I often was, who took the men he wanted, not unwillingly perhaps, but certainly forcefully. And neither of us were man to be taken so.

My own organ was, though, swelling at the sight of him, even fully clothed, and when I saw a movement in the lie of his robe at his center, I smiled to know that he also felt aroused. He circled me as if examining me from all angles, then stopped before me.

"Perhaps we might compare each other's attributes in private," he said, obviously wanting to see what lay beneath my loincloth. "My duty now is to guard my king and his house, but come to me in the morning. At first light come to the barracks of the immortals, and then we shall see who is the greatest of us."

Never had I longed to compare my own organ's size to another's as many men do, but though I was curious about him in that way, I had no great interest in comparing myself to him. For whatever his size, he was as much his king's slave as any slave was, while I was free to roam the world as I pleased.

I laughed. "If you are curious to see if the stories are true, you must wait. I have business here in the morning myself. But tell me this. Are you truly immortal?"

"I serve my king and fight for him as if I were, as do all my men," he replied smiling. "So if you cannot come at dawn, come later . . ."

"Tomorrow I meet your king's first adviser. I have business here on the platform of palaces. But after that . . . after that, who knows what may happen?" I had no desire to offend any man of influence and power.

But he was like a dog with a bone and demanded, "When will your business be done, barbarian?"

"By noon, or not long after."

"Then come after the meal hour. Then I will be rested after guarding my king all night. After I have rested, I will certainly be ready to show you what a true giant is," Mardinaya replied, "and so you do not lose your way, I will have my men escort you from the presence of the first adviser to me." With that, he turned and walked away, back through the doorway he had come from.

I briefly continued my exploration of the platform, but now I had an ache that could not be satisfied by looking at great palaces and temples, and a head full of worry, for my business was serious and dangerous, and I had no desire to be escorted to Mardinaya after it was done, to strut and perform in a useless battle for control.

On my way down the steps, a young man of good build turned his eyes to me in a way I knew. I moved beside him, and he trembled and dropped his eyes. I could have led him to a dark alley close by. But I did not; it would have been like following a puppy to a joining far too gentle for me then.

Chapter Twelve: A Duty Finally Done

I woke with a start, wondering where I was. Then I looked about and knew. I stood and folded my blanket and tossed it by the fire, for I would not need it again; it was now some other man's. Then I took up my weapons and sat by the fire to clean and sharpen them, oiling the leather of the straps and scabbard as well as my quiver. When I was done, I entered the tent of Melioc and Kasra and found them drinking coffee from small cups and ready to leave.

Melioc rose. "Here are the clothes you wanted. Though I still do not understand—"

"All will be clear soon, Melioc old friend. And Kasra; are there fine robes for him too?" I asked smiling at the young man who dropped his eyes, in embarrassed confusion.

"Of course," Melioc answered. "And for me too. A successful merchant and his handsome assistant need to look prosperous, especially when dealing with powerful men."

"Then we go to the public baths," I said and left the tent and headed to where the closed-in donkey cart stood next to it, still with its female in rags huddled inside it.

I undid the door. "We are here lady, in Persepolis, so no more games. I know who you are and you will bathe and then dress as a woman of high rank should and come to the palace with us," I said, holding the bundle of clothing and jewels that Melioc had given me out to her. "And you will join us in our audience with the king's first adviser and tell him why you are here."

For a moment she was silent. Her eyes moved furtively from one to the other of us. "Who sent you?" she asked suspiciously.

"Vivana, the Mede," I replied.

"He did not come himself?"

"He knew I had more chance of arriving safely, lady, and if I do not and he must still come, he will. But no purpose is served if the messenger fails to arrive at his destination as you have," I replied firmly, "So, now, come. Or you will go to the slave markets. Melioc has a right to compensation for rescuing you."

She moved cautiously to the door and stepped out, and after shaking herself, grabbed the bundle of fine clothing and jewels. "I must bathe," she said.

"We all go now to the baths, as we all must bathe," I replied.

"Who is she? Did you know all the time? Why didn't . . . ?" Kasra stammered when we were barely on the road.

"I suspected when I saw the woman's clothing the bandits had in their camp. It was the clothing of a high lady of the Medes, and I knew there was one on the road ahead of me."

"And why . . . ?" Kasra began.

"There will be time enough to know all when our appointment is over," I said. "Melioc, you are quiet."

"Yes. I have heard it whispered that Vivana had a duty to perform that involves me and many other merchants. I am unhappy to come to the notice of powerful men, but . . . one has obligations in our business. That you should be involved, though, has me quite confused."

At the baths the woman Kasra had called Amira, and who still had no other name, was led away while the jewels she was to wear stayed with us. I lay on the stone bench, and my body was oiled and scraped clean, and then I entered the bathing pool. At first I took little notice of the other men there, as I had much on my mind, but then an arrogant and beautiful young man strutted into the chamber.

He stopped where all could see him and languidly raised his arms and stretched his glistening oiled body for the men in the bathing room to see and admire. All heads turned to him, at least briefly, some in admiration, some in envy, and some in long, lingering looks of lust. He languidly lowered his arms, one hand landing on his chest and running slowly, ever so slowly, down his belly through his black curls and on, down to his half-engorged manhood. There his hand lightly wrapped about it and stroked it up, making all eyes focus there as his organ was lifted, as if standing tall, before he released it and stretched again.

I knew that I wanted to take him.

"Dione, come, sit with me," several older men called out, and he finally entered the water near a smiling gray-haired man whose gold bracelets and earrings showed him to be a man of great wealth.

I moved about the pool until I was beside the young man and politely pushed aside his already-panting and slit-eyed old admirer.

"You may have him tomorrow," I said.

The young man looked at me wide eyed and uncertain.

"Who. . . ?"

"Your name is Dione?" I asked.

"Why . . . yes, Dione, but who . . .?"

"I am Konan, a poor barbarian, but I am in need of release, and you are so beautiful I must have you," I replied as I pulled him to me, landing my mouth on his as his ass landed in my lap.

If he had meant to object, my mouth possessing his, my strong hand holding his head to mine and my other strong arm wrapped about his body and pulling him in to me, made it difficult for him to utter any protest. If he punched and kicked at me I did not feel it, and having no doubt he was well used, I quickly had my throbbing organ entering his delicious passage and traveling pleasurably along it with reasonable speed.

His hands soon stopped beating at me, and along with his legs, seemed to wrap about me, rather than kick at me as I continued my journey. And when I arrived at my destination, with my pubic hair rubbing at his ass, he was moaning and showed great interest in continuing the kiss we had begun. I forgot all else but the heat of his body against mine and the wonder of his tight, yet undulating channel caressing my manhood as it moved in and out of him, to our mutual panting and the rising of our seed.

We fountained together in the swirling water of the baths.

When I pulled free of Dione's ass, I felt relaxed and ready to face all I had to do that day, while Dione slumped back against the wall of the pool, spent, his mouth in a sloppy grin and his eyes dazed.

* * * *

Melioc and Kasra had left the bath before Dione arrived and when I joined them had already been massaged, something I no loner needed to relax me, and were dressing in the porticoed courtyard. Melioc was having to help Kasra with some of the ties on the fine robes he was dressing him in. Suddenly young Kasra looked like a grown man, a very handsome one, indeed, and a wealthy one. Melioc was certainly showing his young lover off to his best advantage, and Kasra, knowing how finely he was being dressed, knew it and was smiling happily. Melioc himself was soon looking quite different also, now a mature and wealthy man, and one who had kept his form and strength. His short gray hair stood out also among so many men with black braids and black beards.

I combed my own hair and donned my loincloth and strapped on my weapons and, with Melioc and Kasra following, went to see how the woman was. She stood in the entrance; unrecognizable if I had not known what clothes she had been given. Her hair was glossy and hung in waves down her back under a fine veil, and the fine silks and embroidered edging of her robes highlighted her small, honey-colored hands and sandaled feet. Her face, now it could be seen, was probably pretty, though it was not to my taste. And it was also spoiled by her expression, which was one of suspicion and resentment.

"Kasra calls you Almira," I said to her, "but perhaps it's time you gave us your real name."

"You know who I am barbarian," She replied archly.

"So be it, lady. This is Felthe, concubine to the Prince of the Medes," I said to Melioc and Kasra.

"I am not his concubine. I am his wife," she responded sharply.

"I must have misheard Vivana then, lady," I replied.

Kasra was gaping at her, and by the way his eyes moved over her, I wondered if he was truly satisfied with Melioc. He was young still, and young men can be unsure of their direction and easily led, but he was growing up fast and would eventually find his own way, I was sure. And he was no longer my responsibility. I had brought him to Persepolis as I had promised to.

"Do you still have your seal, Felthe?" I asked.

"What seal?" she asked with suspicious eyes.

"A seal to match this one," I said, holding up the clay marker that I had kept wrapped and hidden these three moons since Vivana had placed it in my hand. "You must have another like this if you are who you claim to be."

"Yes, I have it," she said grudgingly. "But I will only show it when I need to; not to you."

I shrugged and we left he baths and took the road to the platform on which the great palaces of Persepolis stood.

* * * *

"What brings you here, Melioc?" the king Xerxes's first adviser, Atropates, asked the merchant, Melioc, in a friendly manner—after we were led before him and he had greeted us.

"It is not I, but Konan who has sought this meeting, lord," Melioc explained quickly, bowing low and pulling back to remove himself as far as he could from what was to occur next. If he could have, I think he would have run back to his camp, but he was a man of honor.

"Greetings, Atropates, I am Konan, and I come to present the great king Xerxes with the ransom he has demanded for the freedom of Sargon, the man who many know as the Prince of the Medes."

Atropates was silent. And his silence told me the task I had promised to perform was not going to be a simple one.

"Guards," he called, and several very tall and well-muscled, armed men appeared immediately, their long lances in their hands and their short swords at their hips. Things were not progressing well for us.

"These people may need to be escorted to the palace of Xerxes, to meet with our king," he commanded. "But I shall go ahead and speak with my royal master first. You will remain here with them and only follow me when you are ordered to."

"You would make us prisoners . . . ?" the woman, Felthe, cried angrily before Melioc could cover her mouth and silence her, being kicked on the shins for his trouble.

"You are my guests, lady," Atropates replied smoothly as he left.

The guards stood in a circle, watching us with unfriendly and steady eyes.

"What have you got me into?" Melioc mumbled, "Next time I see Vivana I will tell him he may well have spoiled my valuable Persepolis trade."

Kasra simply looked afraid, and Felthe glowered at the guards and ignored us.

* * * *

The woman was harder to control as time went on, and finally I slapped her face, hard. She spat at me.

"If you want to live to see your man, you had better start behaving as a lady should," I told her, "or we will not take you before Xerxes."

"You cannot . . ."

"Yes, I can," I replied. "You are unnecessary to me and are only here because I said you should be. And if we leave you here, Melioc will return and take the fine clothes and jewels that you now wear, but that are Melioc's, and he will have you sold in the slave market to recover the cost of rescuing you and keeping you safe on the journey here."

Felthe glared evilly at me but quieted.

Soon after a man in the robes of a court official hurried in and, with a wave of his arm and a barked "come," the guards herded us along to the palace of Xerxes.

Xerxes was seated on his throne at one end of the hall we entered, and the official led us hurriedly to him. I saw that he was well guarded by tall, strong men, all taller than most Persians. And close beside him stood the giant Mardinaya, who I had met the previous evening, his slitted eyes locked on me as I moved forward.

"Kneel. Bow low," the official hissed to us when we were still several yards from the king.

I dislike kneeling and bowing to any man who has not earned my greatest respect and knelt reluctantly and bowed only as low as I thought would suffice, but I saw movement and suddenly Murdinaya was beside me forcing my head lower. His huge hand on my neck and his powerful fingers digging in to me as he pushed my head down, down, down till it touched the floor. If he sought to prove his strength was greater than mine, he was disappointed, as I did not fight him. I had undertaken a duty to Vivana, the Mede, and was honor bound to place achieving that above all other things. Though I was beginning to feel that Vivana may have asked more of me than he should.

After what seemed a very long time Murdinaya released his grip and I lifted my head and stood, my anger roused but contained.

"I am told you come to ransom him they call Prince of the Medes. What is he to you barbarian?" Xerxes said.

"He is nothing to me, mighty Xerxes," I replied, "but I have promised to undertake a duty for a friend and am here to finish it. Vivana the Mede has sent me with the ransom you demanded. If you accept it, then I have fulfilled my duty and may continue on my journey."

"With the prince no doubt, back to Medea to cause trouble."

"No. I continue my journey to the west." I replied honestly.

"And the prince? What of him once he is free?"

"He is no concern of mine, great Xerxes. I promised to deliver his ransom and see him freed as is the agreement you made. I have no other interest."

Xerxes looked at me long and hard and at the others with me.

"I know you, Melioc, the merchant, but who are the others with you?"

"I am Felthe, wife to the prince," the woman said loudly, raising her chin defiantly. "I also came to ransom him, but . . . but was waylaid by bandits and robbed."

"If you can raise two ransoms for this worthless prince, there seems to be a great deal of wealth in Medea that my tax agents are not collecting," Xerxes replied sharply.

"No, no," Felthe stammered foolishly, "The ransom was not stolen. I . . we . . .we still have it."

"Barbarian, do you understand that I do not want this man free? He has raised people against me when most are happy to be part of my empire and benefit from the peace and prosperity we share. I myself come from the line of the kings of the Medes."

"Mighty Xerxes, I fulfill a promise to a friend, no more. He was duty bound to carry out the task, or see it done, I know no more."

Xerxes sat brooding for some minutes, his dark eyes piercing and his thick black brows hooding his half-closed eyes as he looked at me.

Finally he said. "So be it. There was an agreement. Give me this ransom, and the prince shall go free."

I drew the clay seals from my pouch and unwrapped the one Vivana had given me six moons before. "I need a scribe to write down all that must be paid," I said.

"What is this?" Xerxes said angrily. "Where is my gold? You said you had a ransom for me."

"You shall be paid Xerxes. To you will come all the gold owed to Vivana by the great merchants of the world whose names and debts I shall give to you. When each merchant named is shown this seal I hold, each shall pay what I shall have the scribe record. If any fail to pay, Vivana himself shall make the amount good," I explained. Then there was silence for some minutes before Xerxes spoke again.

"Atropates, tell me what trust I can place in this foolishness."

"Vivana of the Medes is a great merchant of high regard Xerxes, and I know that the merchants often swap what they owe and what is owed to them so they do not carry more gold than is needed on their journeys. So I believe he speaks the truth. But ask Melioc, who you know, for he is a wealthy merchant also. Ask him what he thinks of this."

Melioc stepped forward and replied, "What Atropates says is true. And what the barbarian, Konan, says shall be, shall be, if Vivana has given his accounting of what is due, for he is renowned as a great trader who does business with merchants far and wide and is owed by many of them."

"Tell me the names of these merchants, barbarian, and scribe, take this down," Xerxes said.

"The merchant, Melioc, shall pay 2,600 darius, the merchant Utana 6,700 darius . . ." A gasp went around the hall at such a huge amount. "The merchant Gaubaruva, 11,700 Darius." There was a bigger gasp and much murmuring. "The merchant Arshama 6,000 darius, the merchant Datuvahaya 4,000 darius. That is all."

"What say you, Atropates?" Xerxes asked, still frowning.

"All are noble and wealthy men. I know them all, and all visit Persepolis regularly. All are men whose business would founder if they lost the trust of others. If Vivana says these debts are to be paid to you, then they shall be, Xerxes. Melioc, do you stand good to pay your share now?" Atropates asked.

Melioc stepped forward. "Yes, Atropates. I have a debt to Vivana for trade to Babylon and goods I collected from the Zagros mountains. The gold will come when I sell what I have brought to Persepolis with me. Tomorrow I shall deliver it to Atropates."

"It seems I have been outwitted then. And, woman, how did you intend to pay the ransom."

"I also carried a seal from Vivana," she said.

"Show it to me," Xerxes demanded.

"It is not necessary now," she replied.

"Show me, or I may send you to the barracks to amuse my soldiers."

The woman looked about in confusion. "No, no she stammered," her bravado all gone.

"Show me," Xerxes demanded.

Felthe bent over and lifting her skirts reached up between her thighs and pulled free a small parcel, which she hesitantly unwrapped. It was a seal, but broken, and worthless. She held it out with shaking hands. "I failed," she sobbed.

"It seems that I shall have no choice but to release the Mede. But he shall not return to Ecbatana; he shall go to exile in Thebes, in Egypt. And you, barbarian, shall go with him, as will the woman. Melioc I shall let go free, and this young man," he said indicating Kasra, who had stood wide eyed throughout the days events, "who seems to be of no importance."

"Many thanks, great Xerxes," Melioc said loudly, taking firm hold of Kasra's arm and adding, "and this young man, Kasra, is my heir and will be a fine merchant himself one day, Xerxes."

"Take the barbarian and the woman to join the Medean prince," Xerxes ordered.

At the king's command, Murdinaya and half a dozen of his immortals surrounded us and led us away. The last I saw of Melioc was him standing there looking worried, and my last sight of Kasra was of him with his mouth open, no longer a child, but now a man who understood that the world is a place of uncertainty, where what matters most are ones friends, and lovers, and one's reputation as an honorable man.

Chapter Thirteen: Duty Goes Beyond Persepolis

The Prince of the Mede's, who I had delivered the ransom for on Vivana's behalf, was a handsome man of few morals, great charisma, and even greater ambition. He ranted and raved bitterly at Felthe and me about his coming exile and thanked no one for freeing him, but blamed everyone for his situation and talked openly of escaping and returning to reclaim Ecbatana as his capital.

Felthe had leaped at him when we joined him in his quite comfortable prison, eager to show her love and satisfy his needs, but he seemed to be well satisfied already. Seeing the easy way the guards and the prince spoke to each other, I had some idea of why he may have seemed satisfied.

Felthe had no embarrassment about giving herself to him in front of me, or anyone else. The friendly guards entered regularly and watched what went on, as this was no rough prison but a suite of rooms opening on a high-walled courtyard, the only entrance to which was guarded. The prince also seemed to be quite happy with his couplings with Felthe being observed, and he seemed little interested in her otherwise except for telling her endlessly about returning to Medea and taking his rightful place.

He also made eyes at me, which I ignored. He had caused me and my friends quite enough trouble already, and one of Melioc's men, who had been attacked by the bandits was never likely to walk properly again. From what I saw, though, he was well endowed and had great stamina, a benefit of which was that Felthe was in a happy daze after the first day had ended.

* * * *

The following morning we were taken from the prison and into the courtyard before the palace of Xerxes, and under his eyes, and those of Atropates, we were told that Murdinaya and six of his immortals were to escort us to the town of Berytus, from where the Egyptians would take us to Thebes in Egypt.

On hearing this, the Prince of the Medes threw himself to the ground and railed at Xerxes, theatrically cursing him for sending him into exile. But Xerxes only turned away and left us with Murdinaya and his men.

This was a journey of some distance, I knew, and on foot would have taken perhaps two moons, or more, but in the courtyard were four chariots awaiting us. Large chariots, each taking three people—a driver, a guard, and one of us, the prisoners. I had never ridden in a chariot before and was not keen to enter the one allotted to me, but had no choice.

Murdinaya rode with the Prince of the Medes, and I was glad. The Immortal had given me nothing but looks of arrogant superiority and dislike since I had gone before Xerxes to ransom the prince. And the way he had forced my head to the ground before his king told me that he considered himself greater than me in all ways.

Riding in the chariots made for a fast but bumpy journey. We were able to maintain a good speed, because we changed horses often. We were on King Xerxes's business, and horses awaited us at each official stop, and were freely given, even if there was a shortage. Rarely would so many chariots have arrived at once. Royal messengers might go by chariot, but these were smaller, lighter two-man ones, I discovered.

Once we had left Persepolis several days behind us, we often camped in the open at night, and the giant Persian began to taunt me from that first night.

That first night we stayed in the open I was placed beside the prince and Felthe—who was making up a bed for both of them, while one of the immortals set a fire and baked some vegetables and cooked strips of dried meat for the evening meal. I watched the camp, wary of Murdinaya, who had laid his blanket down but feet away from me and was looking over and leering at me now and then as he cleared the stones from beneath it, as if I were a treat he was about to come for.

Once their beds were made the Persian giant, along with the other men, began cleaning their weapons. Murdinaya stripped off his weapons and his robes and kept only a light short skirt covering his hips and his manhood. I have to say that he was magnificently built, and the prince ogled him openly as Murdinaya smiled at us and stretched in the firelight, showing his fine muscular belly and back, then flexed the muscles of his arms, showing just how strong and well-built he was.

The Prince of the Medes was quite obviously growing in appreciation of the sight before him, and in a moment Felthe was on her knees in front of him with her head under his robe and his organ in her mouth. Even in the fading light of the evening it was plain for all to see what she was doing, and I moved as far from them as I could without seeming to be trying to escape. I had no desire to escape. The chariots we rode in, and the immortals guarding us, all made the journey to Egypt, a place I had desired to visit anyway, much easier for me, and I had no desire to be an enemy of Xerxes, with a price on my head throughout his empire.

Murdinaya saw what was happening, saw the prince's eyes locked on him and the look on the prince's face, and smiled and laughed, giving me a look of disdain. Then he walked up to us, and, looking at me and smiling he said, "It seems your new friend prefers what I have to offer him, barbarian."

The Prince of the Medes sat there gazing up at the Persian giant, with a slack mouth and slitted eyes as Murdinaya dropped the fabric tied about his waist to reveal an already-huge and filling phallus. Grabbing the prince's arm, Murdinaya pulled him to his knees while Felthe scrabbled out from between them, as with his other hand the Persian giant pulled the prince's face to his great manhood.

The Prince of the Medes now had Murdinaya's huge weapon pressed to his lips and greedily opened them to take it in and began eagerly sucking, slurping and moaning on whatever he could get into his mouth of Murdinaya while reaching for his own erect organ and stroking it.

Murdinaya leered at me, and I pulled myself back into the shadows as far as I could, for I would not allow him to see my own arousal. Felthe had pulled back also, confused, and perhaps afraid, but only for a moment, and I could see from her reaction that this was no new thing that was happening.

I admit my eyes had fixed on the Persian's organ and his balls, momentarily unsure if he or I was bigger and for the first time ever feeling a small part of what other men must feel when I revealed myself to them, and yes, feeling other urges.

Meanwhile, one of Murdinaya's men moved in and pulled Felthe away, and as the prince licked and sucked eagerly on the Persian giant's tool and fondled his ball sack, I glanced over and saw her pushed onto her back with her legs splayed and bent and held down as another of our guards removed the short wrap he'd had about his hips and entered her and began to ride her. After struggling briefly when she was being pulled away from her lover, she quickly gave signs of enjoying the ride, moaning and even urging them on. Meanwhile, her husband or lover—I was uncertain what to believe, doubting both the prince's and her truthfulness about anything—was fully occupied in sucking on what of Murdinaya's great organ he could get into his mouth.

I ignored what was happening as well as I could. For I was sure that if I made any sign of joining in, Murdinaya would be upon me. One of his men, the youngest I thought he was, had moved up as if to join him but instead pulled the prince's hips up and, getting down behind him, parted his checks and began to tongue his hole as the prince writhed and moaned louder and sucked more eagerly. Soon fingers were being worked into the prince's hole as the prince began to move his hips. And then the young Persian spread his thighs and pulled the prince's ass between them, guiding his own moderate-size organ to the prince's hole, and entering him. The prince moaned and clawed at Murdinaya's hips and ass as the giant slowly moved his head back and forth on his now fully erect organ, though the prince could only take a part of its great length.

The sound of taking and the sight of Murdinaya and his companion working on the prince and raising his hips and working on his entrance had inflamed me, but Murdinaya had looked over at me with a wicked smile on his face, and I refused to let him see me give myself release. Instead, I pretended to be busy getting stones out from under my blanket and turned away and shut my ears and meditated on the future.

"My great size has frightened the barbarian," I heard Murdinaya say between his grunts and murmurs, and if I had disliked him before, I now knew there could never be any trust or friendliness between us.

And while I could avoid watching the two Persians take the prince, after a while hearing him suddenly crying out and suspecting what had happened, I was not able to stop myself turning and seeing that now it was the Persian giant who knelt behind the Mede, moving his huge throbbing weapon into the prince's lubricated and opened hole as the prince pressed his chest into the dirt and spread his thighs wider, trying desperately to open and widen himself more to accommodate what was making its way inside him.

The prince's cries of being taken finally turned to moans and grunts and later still to demands for "more,

more," and I knew he had accommodated the giant and now shared the ride completely. Looking toward Felthe, I had seen that she eagerly moved herself into various positions as several of the men took their turn with her. Glancing toward either of them was unavoidable at times, for both were eager and noisy partners, and I was racked by a throbbing need I could not release. When Murdinaya and his companion were finally done with the prince, Felthe pulled away from the men she was with and returned to him, now naked for all to see, and fell to licking his body clean of his and Murdinaya's seed.

The other immortals looked on, and some worked on their own tools, while others, who had enjoyed her already, merely watched while they cleaned their weapons. Apparently Murdinaya's behavior was no surprise to them. And the looks that several directed at me had me nervous that he might have his men assist him to take me if he chose to do that forcefully. I had no desire to be fighting them all off.

When we had eaten and the camp finally slept. I was at last able to give myself release but had to bury my head in my blanket so the Persian giant snoring but a few yards from me did not hear.

Whenever we camped in the open, Murdinaya would ensure I knew he was a man of great size and stamina and would leer at me and laugh while taking great pride in stretching and showing his great height and his bulky muscles and that great log hanging between his thighs and already giving signs of filling out. And he made a point of ensuring that I always had a good view of him when he used that tree trunk of a phallus inside another.

I was annoyed that I could not ignore him as he tried each day to show how much stronger and bigger than me he was. And how much more noble and proud he had a right to be. I knew he was none of those things. So why couldn't I ignore him?

He also liked to show how much power he had over the prince as if it mattered to me, which it fortunately did not, or I may not have been able to restrain myself.

The next time we camped in the open, and after we had eaten and he had checked the camp was secure and set the guards, he approached the prince, leering at me as he did so, and whispered to the prince who smiled and nodded his head. He then pulled Felthe to him and with little preparation pushed her back and lifted her robe and entered her. When he had ridden her a brief while, he withdrew though she tried to pull him back, and pulled her up and turned her away from him and running his hands under her robe grasped her breasts lifting her robe above her waist and Murdinaya moved between her thighs. She did not hesitate to wrap her legs about his hips but cried out when he entered her, and she grunted and gasped loudly with each deep stroke he made into her. When he'd had enough of her, he withdrew, and the prince pushed her down onto her hands and knees and entered her from behind—and then it was obvious what had been planned, as the Persian knelt behind the prince and after some preparation entered him, so that the prince was caught between his two lovers and made a great noise in showing his pleasure at the arrangement.

When we rested in the day, it was soon common for any man who needed release to take it with Felthe as the prince looked on, with obvious enjoyment.

One day I said to Felthe, "What sort of marriage is yours where your husband willing shares you with other men?"

"One that suits me very well, barbarian. I like it, and how many husbands would want a wife who enjoys what I do?" she replied

"Few," I replied.

"Most would beat me if they even guessed what I might enjoy. And to share just one man with other wives? Ha. I am the luckiest of women, barbarian, to have the man I have, whatever sort of vain and stupid dreamer he is."

And I understood her at last.

Chapter Fourteen: A New Journey Begins

We had reached Berytus and the Prince of the Medes, Felthe, and I had been passed over to the Egyptians. The local governor had met us at his house and, while looking unhappy, had given a speech of welcome to Murdinaya that would please Xerxes when it was taken back to him.

And once we had been passed over we were sent to the cells. The accommodation provided to the Prince of the Medes by the governor was not so comfortable as that provided to him by Xerxes in Persepolis. And the door of the cell was not even closed on us before the prince was again loudly moaning of his right to better things and his complaints—his moans on the journey having been largely confined to the ones he made as the giant Persian immortal, Murdinaya, plowed him.

Murdinaya was not there now, and I was about to explode from the scorching fires of unsatisfied need that had been smoldering in me for the many days of the journey. I removed my weapons and my loincloth and set them safely aside. The prince barely had time to open his eyes in surprise before Felthe gasped and the prince cried out in fear as I grabbed him and threw him roughly onto one of the narrow beds.

I knew he had been well used by the giant the night before, his cries and moans had been all too clear as I lay in a bed in the same room, gritting my teeth and staring at the wall, trying to ignore Murdinaya making a show of his last wild taking of the prince and his concubine.

One mighty grasp and tear of the fabric of his robes had the so-called Prince of the Medes naked, shaking fearfully, and covering himself with his hands. "I . . . I . . . I had no choice but to lie with him," he blabbered. "Tell them in Medea that I had no choice. He would have forced me otherwise, and I discovered secrets from him. Tell them in Medea when we return, tell them that. For it's true. I have to do things I do not wish to do to survive and return to my people, barbarian. Vivana will understand."

"I doubt Murdinaya would be pleased to hear you talk so," I said with a laugh, almost wishing the giant Persian were there with us to hear the prince's lies.

"Cloth to bind him, Felthe," I said.

She looked at me with big eyes but hurried to tear a shawl she had into strips and handed them to me. The prince struggled to get up and tried to escape my grip but was too weak to do so.

"You are a liar and a fool, prince, and I have no idea why Vivana—a good and honest man—would risk anything for you."

"Vivana," he spat out angrily in spite of his fear. "That disloyal fraud. On his deathbed my father begged him to fund my campaign when I had half of Medea in my hands and only needed to take Ecbatana; but Vivana refused. All he would promise my father—who he claimed he loved, ha— was to try to help me. And my poor foolish father believed him and went to his grave content. Years they were lovers and friends, but Vivana never treated me as family."

"A wise man," I replied as I finished binding his hands to the bed frame. and the prince kicked at me and writhed as he complained about better men and lied about lying with the Persian. And I grew hard knowing what was to come. Finally, I had both his wrists and his ankles secured, and all he could do was lurch and writhe about and lift his ass into the air. An agreeable situation.

I got onto the bed and straddled him, and grasping his waist roughly, lifted his ass up to a comfortable height. Wrapping an arm about his belly, I held him there in spite of his efforts to escape me, and I plunged several fingers of my other hand in his hole, which made him scream loudly, though it felt loose to me. "Oil," I called out to Felthe. She had seen the small oil pot by my things and hurried to pass it to me. I was very generous in oiling up his ass while remembering the nights he had eagerly and loudly lain with the Persian giant and the days when he had flirted and laughed with him, always in front of me.

I made only a brief effort to open him though ensuring he was well and deeply oiled. Then I guided the head of my throbbing cock to his entrance and, with a great sigh of finally accomplishing something worthwhile, I entered him—as he screamed and struggled. His protests were music to my ears, and I entered him as quickly as I could, I admit. And soon I bottomed deep inside him. I briefly wondered if I should ask him if I had reached deeper than the Persian giant, but from his screams of violation, I was sure I had—and the prince was in my opinion not worth asking anything. I glanced over and saw Felthe wide-eyed and lifting her skirt up and rubbing herself. At least she was honest about her tastes and pretended to be nothing but what she was.

"A woman such as you can make a great deal of gold doing what she enjoys," I said to her, and she looked shocked.

Having gone to the depths of the prince, now I plowed him, but not too long, because all my pent up heat had me ready to explode at the mere feel of a warm channel encasing me after so many days of nothing but my own hands in the darkness. My cream spouted out of me in great spasms, and gave me some relief, but I did not pull out of the prince then. I did not want to. I wanted to ride his ass again and again, but I made myself pull out. I was aching for more, but I did not want to tire myself.

I got off him and left him tied up there while I lay on one of the other beds.

"Is that all you can manage?" Felthe asked, with disappointment in her voice.

"The day is young, Felthe. Be patient," I replied and lay there listening.

Soon there were noises and the door to our cell was opened, but it was not the one I expected. "Barbarian," the guard standing there said, "follow me."

I left the cell and followed him along the corridor to a guardroom, where the Egyptian governor waited nervously.

"The immortal, Murdinaya, has tried to bribe my guards to allow him to enter your cell, barbarian. I don't wish to anger Xerxes, and I do not know what Murdinaya may want to do once inside, so I ask you now if you know what is going on. Murdinaya has had plenty of opportunity to remove the prince while journeying here, and I have no desire to be accused of doing that myself if he dies in my cells."

"Murdinaya seeks to come to our cell for me, not for the prince, and I doubt he would come alone," I added.

"He wanted access for two men. What is this about?"

"He seeks to make me bow before him," I replied. "He has been itching to prove himself a greater man than I since the moment we met, and I have given him no opportunity. I kneel to no man I do not admire and honor, and surrounded by his men, I had little hope of making him kneel to me. Let him come; I am ready for him. And you may be assured he will leave here alive," I said.

The governor looked at me long and hard. "I have heard you were the one who brought the ransom to Xerxes, no more. The prince was not worth ransoming, but Xerxes likes gold and foolishly set a price. When the Persians leave, you may go free, but only if Murdinaya leaves here alive and knowing nothing of this conversation."

"So be it. Have your men ready to see what happens, so they may vouch to you for what occurs when he comes."

I returned to the cell and lay there waiting. Felthe understood enough to know there was more to come and sat on her own narrow bed with a small smile on her lips.

"You say there is money to be made by a woman like me, barbarian. I have heard of such things and will think on it."

Finally, there was a rustling noise, and the cell door was opening again.

I was there in an instant and barely had time to see Murdinaya smiling an evil smile, before I had yanked him inside and landed a foot in his belly that drove his younger companion back into the passage as I closed the cell door. Then I leaped, and my two feet landed square on Murdinaya's belly and he toppled back to the floor, gasping for air and clutching at himself. If I heard the door's outer bolt being slid over I had no time to wonder at the efficiency of the governor's guards in ensuring that it was to be a fair fight.

Felthe was there with the remaining strips of her shawl, and in a moment I had the giant's hands bound together while he recovered his breath.

"What, barbarian," he roared angrily as he twisted from under me. "You would challenge me? I am Murdinaya, greatest of the immortals. Famed throughout the world."

"Famed throughout Xerxes's world," I grunted as I wrestled him there on the cell floor.

We tore at each other's clothes and bodies, seeking to find a grip. My loincloth was gone in moments, and Murdinaya's own robes were also soon gone as we rolled about, so that we wrestled naked. Even though his hands were tied, he was challenging my strength. He was trained to fight. His life was no more than to fight for Xerxes, and he knew many tricks. His body was oiled also, I discovered, and slipped from my hands as I tried to grab his arms and legs and tip him over or hold him down. As we ground our skin together, though, the oil spread over my skin also, and soon he was as unable as I to hold a grip or keep his legs wrapped about mine to still them.

Now our bodies were pressed together I could feel his hardness. I knew I was stronger and larger, but he knew fighting skills I was yet ignorant of, so we were well matched. Somehow he got up on my back to the delighted cries of the watching prince, who struggled with his bonds and shouted at Felthe to free him.

I tried to clamp my legs around Murdinaya but was tipped off him yet again, and we fell and wrestled chest to chest, legs twining and untwining, belly to belly, hard cock rubbing hard cock, for some time before I finally moved him about and got an arm around his neck and pulled his head back and sat on his back. He scrabbled hard, but with his hands tied, he was trapped at last. Our breath came in rough gasps, and sweat and oil made our bodies slick. My manhood ached, and with his ass beneath me at last, I wanted nothing more than to part his cheeks and expose his hole so I could enter him. But I had only two hands to hold him, and if I stopped sitting on him . . . he gave a mighty lurch and freed a leg and I was struggling to regain control. We wrestled on, though he never again took complete control, and soon he tired. He was used to an easy victory. He may have trained well, but he had not walked half the world as I had and lacked true stamina.

When I had him on his knees with my legs wrapped in a tight grip about his chest and my arms parting his legs to expose his hole, my rock hard pole seemed to be magically guided to that puckered and twitching entrance and rested a moment at his rim. I did not hesitate. I pushed my hips down and back and gained entrance. Only a short way, barely inside his rim, but I had entrance. He screamed and cried his outrage and tried harder to wriggle free, but his wriggling only succeeded in allowing my pole to enter him further, which led to more bucking and kicking from him, which by the generosity of the gods, let me sink even deeper into his channel.

Murdinaya's ass was tight, and if another man had been up there, he hadn't left his mark. So perhaps I was the first. I was certainly the one who plowed him deepest. I rode his ass while he lurched and bucked so that working my manhood in him in that position was like riding a wild beast. When I came, I roared loudly, feeling a true release at last. Then I saw the prince looking on and humping the bed beneath him with a hard weapon of his own. I reached under the Persian and felt his organ was hard and that his hips were moving up and down involuntarily as he stroked the side of the head of his phallus against the floor of the cell.

"Felthe," I said, "the fabric."

Murdinaya lurched mightily and tried to dislodge me. But my cock held its place inside him and my legs tightened about his belly and my hands gripped his ankles harder. And still I rode him, though with a mighty effort, he lifted his chest and arms from the ground only to sink back when he felt the difference tightening his ass on my buried pole made to him. Weakened by our struggling he landed with a grunt, and his arms trembled and gave way and his chest fell to the ground as he shook with rage and frustration at his situation.

Felthe hurried up and was tying his ankles to his wrists without my even telling her to. The prince suddenly saw this and cried, "No, Felthe, no, he is my friend. Tie the barbarian instead." Felthe hesitated and looked at me appraisingly.

"What waits for us in Egypt?" she asked.

"Whatever you or the prince is clever enough to get for you," I replied. "If he pleases those he is being sent to, you will live well, if not, then . . ."

She looked over at the prince and hesitated.

"Untie Murdinaya, then me, you fool," the prince cried.

"I doubt the Egyptians will like my prince," she said softly. "The Persians did not," and with that she finished binding Murdinaya's ankles to his wrists as the prince shouted abuse at her and increased his struggles.

Now I could mount the great Persian giant as I chose, and I rode him like a dog, knowing that I could ride him through the night. Ride him as I chose. And soon he came with a good flow of his own and wailed in his ecstasy at the coming and the agony of knowing who had ridden him to it.

I roared with increasing satisfaction as I spouted yet another flow inside him, marking him as beaten and marking him as mine. I could have ridden him till dawn, but before then Egyptian guards entered the cell and pulled me off the immortal Persian and took him away, half carrying him as he was barely able to stand unaided and whimpered and cried to the gods to punish me and swore to see me dead.

As I was not yet done I straddled the prince again and rode him a good while till the last small spouting saw me empty of frustration and anger and relieved of the ache I had felt for so many days. And then I slept.

When I awoke, Felthe and the prince were gone and the cell door was open. I put on my loincloth and my weapons and left.

"You are free to go, barbarian, but only if you do not take the road back the way you came. You have made a mortal enemy of the Persian giant, in fact of all Persians. For Xerxes does not want you free either," the governor said.

"I am happy to go on to Egypt," I replied, "for it is a land I have heard much of, and have long wanted to visit."

The governor shrugged. "I am sure you will be welcomed by some, barbarian, but perhaps not by others," he added with a smile. "Your reputation will certainly go before you this time. And I doubt the prince will have any good to say of you."

"Men tell many stories of me," I replied with a smile.

Epilogue: Another Journey Begins

I was frightened when I saw the Persians take Konan and the prince and Felthe away, and was glad that Melioc hurried us out of the palace.

Persepolis seemed to be a very dangerous place to be an honest man and I was grateful that I had a protector. If I had been with Konan still . . .

"Why did Konan do such a dangerous thing for this Vivana?" I asked quietly as we hurried back to where Melioc had his camp.

"I doubt he knew it was so dangerous when he agreed to do it."

"But he must have had a great love for Vivana to say he would," I murmured, feeling hurt. "What is Vivana like? Is he young and handsome?"

Melioc laughed a short laugh, for he gave every sign of being worried, "Vivana is as old as I am, if not older. But he is a man who takes on challenges and a man with a great passion for men who will take him roughly and deeply, and I am sure none have done that as well as Konan did.

"Konan did not love you less, Kasra," Melioc continued, stopping and turning to me. "He asked me once what I had to offer you, when I complained that he hurt you when he left you alone while he took his pleasure with other men. He reminded me that I have had many young men join me in my tent and few have lasted more than a journey or two and that I have turned many over for a handsomer one I found walking by the road, with no thought for the one I left behind. He said he had promised to protect you and deliver you to your uncle. Then when he knew you wanted more than your old home could offer and that you had no uncle to give it to you, and . . . and that you had some small liking for me, he asked me again what I was willing to offer you. I told him then that if you came to me I would make you my heir. And then he brought you to my tent and we . . . I took you as my lover and you were mine."

I looked at Melioc and knew what he said was true and that I could not have shared the wild and dangerous life Konan had. And I understood too that the barbarian had loved me enough to give me what was best for me, which was a great thing. I embraced Melioc. "He did well for me," I said, and we hurried back to his tent so I could show him how glad I was with what I now had.

Sabb

Once an accountant and sometime property developer, Sabb is a wild barbarian at heart. He lives by a lake on Australia's east coast where he enjoys the gym and shares his home with dogs. Many dogs. He also writes and has been published under other names in other genres. He co writes gay erotica with habu, as Shabbu, and non-erotic gay romance with habu, as Stephen Kessel.

Not all books listed below may currently be in print release.
BOOKS BY DIRK HESSIAN
Blue and Gray
Colonel's Treasure
Beginning of Time
Prophecy of Noto
The King's Men
Labyrinth
BOOKS BY HABU
13 Ways for Halloween (Menage)
The Indian Prince
The Handyman
Grab Bag
Cairo Surrender
Fetish Galore!

Homeward Bound
Journey to Mirage
Choke Hold
Sporting Life
BOOKS BY SHABBU
Dirty Pool
Operation Black Jade
Yap, Yap
Cigars!
Angel in the Barn
Gayly Complicated
Despoiling David
The Tree of Idleness
Rough Road to Happiness
I Met a Man
The Interview
Rough Road to Happiness
BOOKS BY SABB
The Legend of Holleystone Grange
Surprise Encounters
She is He
Wrong Man
Loyal to his King
Barbarian Tales - Book One - Traveler's Tales
Barbarian Tales - Book Two - Journeys Begin
Barbarian Tales - Book Three - The Inheritance
Barbarian Tales - Book Four - Road to Persepolis

~